Purushothama

The King Who Defied The Great

Purushothama

The king who defied the great

- Adhi Vishnu

Author's Note

History, as we know it, is often written by the victors—or at least, by those whose voices carried across the centuries. The Battle of Hydaspes, fought between King Porus of the Pauravas and Alexander of Macedon, is one such event where the truth remains obscured.

The records we have today are almost entirely from Greek sources—writers like Arrian, Plutarch, and Curtius—men who never fought on that battlefield but sought to preserve Alexander's glory. According to their accounts, Alexander triumphed and Porus was made his vassal. Yet from the Indian tradition, faint but persistent across time, lingers another memory: that Porus did not fall, that he fought with such ferocity and won the admiration of his foe, perhaps even drove the Macedonians back.

There is no single clear evidence of how that war truly unfolded. This ambiguity left a silence in history—and it is in that silence that imagination can take root.

I chose to write this story not as the Greeks told it, but from the Indian perspective, where Porus stands not just as a footnote in Alexander's conquest, but as the *defender who defied the greatest conqueror the West ever produced* . To Aryavarta, Porus was not the defeated—he was the king who fought for his people, his dharma, his land, and won in ways deeper than victory or defeat can capture.

This retelling is my tribute to that perspective: to give voice to Porus, to the nameless warriors who stood and fell on those muddy banks of the Hydaspes. For history may remember Alexander as a world conqueror, but it must also remember that here, at the edge of India, he was stopped by a king who refused to break.

In blending fact, myth, and imagination, I wished to honor that silent victory, to reframe the Hydaspes not as Alexander's inevitability, but as Porus' endurance and Aryavarta's defiance. This is not history as written—but history as remembered, as reimagined, and as it deserves to be told.

—Ledalla Naga Sai Adhi Vishnu

Preface

The Battle of Hydaspes, fought between King Porus of the Pauravas and Alexander of Macedon, remains one of history's great enigmas. The truth of what unfolded on those riverbanks has been blurred by time and perspective. What we know comes almost entirely from Greek historians such as Arrian, Plutarch, and Curtius, who wrote in praise of Alexander's greatness. Yet in India, faint traditions and folk memories tell a different tale—that Porus stood as a true king, unyielding before the world's greatest conqueror, and may have even turned him back.

This book was born from that silence between perspectives. With no definitive Indian record of the war, imagination must step in where history does not speak. Rather than attempting to reconstruct facts, I have chosen to reimagine—to tell this story as a novel, not as a chronicle of dates and measured events. For that reason, you will not find rigid timelines, precise troop movements, or recorded speeches here. What you will find is the *essence* of the war: its terror and valor, its betrayals and loyalties, and the spirit of a land that refused to bow.

I have written this not as a history textbook, but as a story—meant to be lived, felt, and experienced through its characters. By leaving aside exact dates and figures, I wanted to create space for readers to hear the roar of elephants, to see the clash of warriors, and to breathe the uncertainty of men who knew they might not see another dawn.

In these pages, Porus is not a forgotten name in Alexander's annals, but a voice of resistance, honor, and compassion. My hope is that readers will meet him not as history reduced him, but as he might have been remembered by his people—King Purushottama, the king who defied the Great.

—Ledalla Naga Sai Adhi Vishnu

Table of Content:

Uttarapatha Route & Hydaspes Battle (326 BCE)

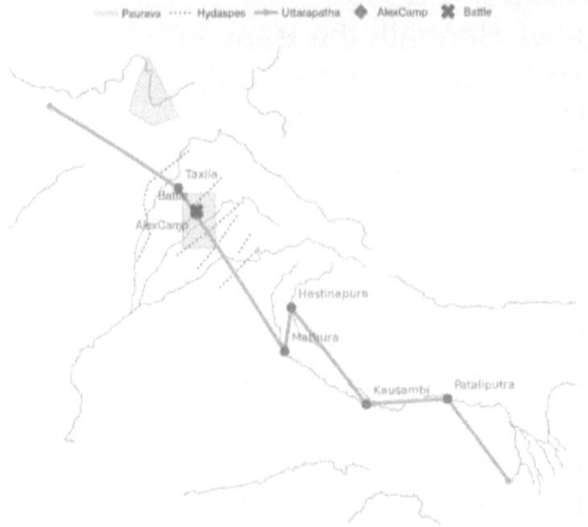

Chapter 1: When the Walls Breathed Gold

The golden rim of dawn crept slowly over the eastern horizon, washing the sandstone walls of the city in muted fire. Towering and impenetrable, the ancient fortress of the Paurava kingdom rose like a watchful titan from the fertile plains—not merely a structure of security, but a symbol of discipline, pride, and enduring legacy.

Only a single gate opened into this citadel— a deliberate design , crafted for both defense and control. At its arch, guards clad in polished chainmail stood like sculptures of vigilance, checking each arrival with disciplined precision. Every person entering the city—

whether local or foreign—was required to present a token of passage , an insignia issued by the royal court or approved trader guilds. No token, no entry. No exception.

A caravan waited at the threshold, its camels burdened with fabric from far-off Bactria and tubs of resin wrapped in thick wool. Their owners, wrapped in dust-colored robes, spoke a northern dialect, their breath steaming in the cool morning light. One of them bowed slightly, offering a golden-threaded scroll as his permit. The guards inspected it, nodded wordlessly, and stepped aside. The camels groaned as they entered.

Inside the capital, the city was already awakening. It was not a clumsy sprawl of homes but a carefully tiered world , divided by walls within walls— three great sectors , each pulsing with its own rhythm of life.

Sector One

The outermost ring, closest to the main gate, belonged to the workers . Streets buzzed with craftsmen hammering copper, weavers setting up looms, women grinding herbs, children darting through alleyways with eyes full of dust and dreams. The bazaar was coming alive. Stalls sprang open like flowers—spices spilled over earthen bowls, brass ornaments caught the early sun, and the air soon filled with scents of warm milk, cardamom, and sandalwood oil.

This was where the city's pulse beat loudest: raw, busy, essential.

Sector Two

Beyond the first wall, through a guarded checkpoint, lay the **middle tier** —where palace clerks, minor officials, priests, and mid-tier merchants made their lives. Straight roads lined with flowering neem trees guided one past double-storied homes, modest gardens, and statues of local deities veiled in silk. These were people of order, bookkeepers of the realm, men and women whose hands held ink as often as gold. Couriers rushed toward the citadel, delivering sealed sheets and stamped wax—words were power here.

Sector Three

The innermost sanctum, protected by high towers and elite guards, was a world of its own. The **royals, commanders, noble houses, and the king himself** resided here. Painted courtyards, stone elephants, and water-lily ponds adorned this elevated realm. From the grand court hall, decisions rippled outward—shaping tax, trade, alliances, and war. The smell here was not of sweat and copper, but of myrrh and cedar, of gold rubbed with rosewater.

And yet, unlike distant empires, this city was not trapped in its own hierarchy. Advancement was no illusion. One could climb, and many had. The artisan's child could become the royal architect. A spice seller's son might earn his scroll and advise kings— merit moved faster than birth.

As Morning Unfolded....

Trade was the breath of the city, and the city had begun to inhale. Foreigners from Persia and Kamboja, from the Tamil coast and Scythian steppes, all strolled into the square, each bearing goods and stories. They traded silks for salt, lapis for cotton, spices for scrolls . Deals were swift but fair—every transaction was a dance where profit walked beside pride.

The educators , too, had begun their day. Across all three sectors, rang the soft chants from Gurukuls , where children gathered before stone idols or under sacred trees to study everything from scriptures and logic to astronomy and martial arts. Birthplace meant little here. Interest and dedication decided which child would learn medicine, which would learn trade, which would hold a sword.

As the sun lifted higher, golden banners with the crest of the Paurava king caught the light. Somewhere deep within the third sector, the royal palace gates rumbled open. A priest entered, bearing a fresh omen. Ministers gathered. Scrolls awaited signatures.

But in the city below, no one saw the omen, nor the messenger, nor the faint unease with which the royal priest walked.

The stalls opened. Bells rang. Horses neighed. All was as it had always been—peaceful, loud, alive.

And far away—beyond the river Vitasta (Hydespes) , beyond the hills, beyond even the knowing of maps— a shadow stirred.

Chapter 2: The Lion Within the Wall

The hour of the second prahar had come. The sun shone low but bright above the eastern ramparts of the city, throwing long shadows across the stone walls of the Paurava palace fortress. Inside the royal compound, soldiers stood posted at every archway and stair. Towering walls of ancient brick, reinforced over generations, surrounded the inner sanctum—imposing yet stirred with beauty.

At the heart of it all stood the royal darbar hall—not simply a court of law and governance, but the chamber where history itself took form.

Its high ceilings arched above in graceful curves, upheld by massive stone pillars etched with lotus vines and battle scenes. Sunlight filtered through colored glass insets, painting the marble floor in shifting patterns. The air was heavy with sandalwood and crushed jasmine; incense trailed up through the dome like prayers toward heaven.

The central carpet, deep crimson with golden borders, cut a direct path from the great double doors to the king's dais. Flanking the carpet on both sides stood ten finely carved high seats, raised slightly above smaller benches for court officers and scribes. Behind them, two tiers of wide stone steps circled the rear of the chamber—a gallery open to common citizens, where any man, woman, or child was welcome to witness the court's proceedings.

This was Purushothama's design—the king who believed that a throne without the eyes of the people was a chair in a dark room.

The ministers had already arrived.

Men of varying age and build stood by their seats—some scholars, some warriors, some merchants now elevated to councilors. Their conversation died into reverent silence as the blast of a conch echoed through the vaulted chamber.

The great teak doors opened with a solemn groan.

And in walked the king.

Born of iron and earth, Purushothama, king of Paurava, known among foreigners as Purushottama, stood taller than most men by a head. His skin carried the hue of thickened rain clouds; his body was forged not in rest-houses, but on horseback and in war camps. Thick, dark hair trailed behind his shoulders, and his cheekbones stood like twin ridgelines above a steady, commanding gaze—brown eyes flecked with gold.

There was no rustle of silk or fanfare of jewels. He wore only a short tunic of white, a leather-warrior girdle, and a royal sash of indigo wrapped across his chest. Around his left wrist was a single gold armlet, shaped like a roaring lion—the mark of his dynasty.

He ascended the steps of the golden throne, its arms formed from twin elephant heads and its back plate adorned with the embossed insignia of the kingdom: a rising sun, bisected by a river, flanked by two lances.

He sat, slowly, and silence spread like mist.

The first to rise was Vartraya, the minister of trade and internal commerce. Dressed in plain robes but silver-witted, he raised a scroll in both hands.

"Maharaja, greetings of the second moon. I bring reports from the southern gates, the temple bazaars, and our northern trade stations."

Purushothama gave a single nod.

Vartraya adjusted his scroll.

"Over the last three lunar cycles, the inflow of trade has grown by thirty-seven percent. Merchants from Gandhara continue to seek our perfumes, dyes, and silks. Traders from

Kalinga offered coastal pearls in exchange for Paurava iron. Two caravans from the Yavana lands—"
He looked briefly at the foreign envoy seated in shadow.
"—have expressed interest in our gemstones, indigo blocks, and mechanical water-lifting devices."
A murmur of pride swept through the chamber. The city was thriving. The treasury chambers were full.
Then, a shift in tone.
"Yet trouble brews from the northwest. Ambhi, king of Taxila, son of the late Ambhiraja, has increased unauthorized tolls on northern roads. Traders seeking a short route through his domain report extortion, harassment... even robbery."
There was no uproar. Only stillness.
Until Senapati Ashmaka, the commander of frontier patrols, stood.
"These are not bandits, Maharaja. Our intelligence shows these are disguised Taxilan soldiers, stationed off-route in the forests. They intercept carts bearing our royal insignia—likely in an attempt to force traders northward."
The air tightened.
Raja Guru Devadatta, the oldest among the court—clad in white, his beard to his chest—rose with folded hands.
"Your Majesty, shall I remind the court what blood was spilled before this shadow rose?"
"It was not long ago that your lord's blade slew Ambhiraja—your uncle, your wife's father, and former lord of Takshashila."
Heads turned toward the raja guru. Even seasoned ministers shifted uneasily.
"He who betrayed the Paurava flag in secrecy and silence. He who invited foreign swords into our temples."
Purushothama's fingers gently closed around the armrest of his throne.
Silence.
Then, the king's voice rang low and steady:

"Justice is not mercy. Ambhiraja sold our soil for coin and pride. I returned it with fire."
He leaned forward slightly, gaze fixed straight.
"If his son now wears his hate, let him wear the consequences too."
Ashmaka looked up from his notes.
"Ambhi grows bold. His spies are clever, his gold farther-reaching than we thought. Shall we send scouts deeper into his borderlands?"
The king shook his head once.
"If he conspires war, he'll show his teeth soon enough."
Raja Guru stepped beside the throne.
"Still, Maharaja, you must know... the vultures watch. The Malavas sway like reeds, the Gandharas hold cold smiles, the Dhanava princes of Vidisha ask questions we don't wish to answer."
"Yet," he added, "Kalinga holds firm. And a word from the Ganga plain suggests Magadha watches with interest in our strength."
Purushothama exhaled through his nose.
"Good. Then let them keep watching."

From the Outer Roads

As small matters were raised—soil issues in southern villages, a dispute over temple lands, oxen seized by tax collectors in error—the king passed judgment swiftly, but thoughtfully. Resolve, repay, replace—all in order.
And then—
The tall doors creaked open once more.
A soldier, face weary from days of travel, dirt crusting his brow, strode in. Behind him, a courier on foot held a sealed scroll dark as night, marked with black wax—no kingdom's symbol, no scribe's crest.
He dropped to one knee, heart pounding.
"Forgive me, Maharaj..."

A pause. His voice cracked.
"...It came from the Sindhu border garrisons, just before dawn."
Purushothama accepted the scroll in silence.
The wax seal was unmarked—but deeply scored, as though something had clawed over it.
"No sign from west or east," the soldier whispered. "But something moves beyond the mists... something not our own."
The king stood. The court fell still.

Chapter 3: A Scroll from the West

The wind that followed the messenger into the royal court was warm, dry, and eerie—as if it had crossed a desert no one dared name.

He entered through the stone-carved gates of the Paurava Darbar Hall, his breath uneven, eyes wide, forehead streaked with dust and dried sweat. His clothing, though marked with the kingdom's insignia, was torn near the hem, and his leather sandals thudded on the marble floor with hurried steps. It took only moments for everyone gathered to sense that the man had seen something far greater than he could carry within his bones.

Even in the presence of his king—Purushothama—the messenger did not bow at first. He stood frozen, gazing at the marble lions, then at the rows of royal court members, before locking eyes momentarily with the throne. There, seated like time clothed in human form, sat the king—broad-shouldered, unflinching, unmoved.

But even Purushottama's watchful eyes narrowed slightly.

He could see it.

The fear.

"You carry a scroll?" asked the court officer seated nearest to the stairs.

The messenger nodded slowly, outstretching a trembling hand. "From… across the Indus," he said, breath shaky. "A force… like I've never seen, Maharaj. The gods themselves—"

"Scroll," the officer interrupted softly, taking it.

The messenger nodded hurriedly, still trembling.

The officer handed it to Raja Guru Devadatta, who inspected it closely—the seal was foreign: a circular emblem bearing a lion crossing a serpent, with markings carved in a script unfamiliar to most. Devadatta's brows drew close.

"This... is not Persian. This is... Greek."

Then, without a word more, the raja guru turned and handed the parchment to the Greek officer who had served in the court for years—a former foreigner turned ally, one who knew both tongues, both worlds.
The hall fell silent.
The Greek unrolled it slowly, and what he saw made the blood drain from his face.
Only one line was carved in bold, militant script. He read it. And then read it again.
Trembling, he turned to the king and his guru, voice cracking.
"O King... the scroll reads:
Be ready for war.
...And it bears the royal seal of Alexander."
The silence in the darbar hall was like a held breath.
"One of the younger commanders gripped his sword hilt too tightly. An older noble quietly mouthed a prayer to Indra."
Purushottama leaned forward atop his golden throne, the shadows between his fingers growing long.
"War?" he said softly. "With whom?"
The Greek officer swallowed.
"Alexander. Son of Philip. King of Macedon. Conqueror of Egypt. Liberator of Babylon. Lord of Persia. He now moves east, toward our land."
The messenger stepped forward, his voice now steadier. "I bring no myth, Maharaj… I bring what I saw."
The court leaned into his words.
"He camps beyond the river Sindhu, with an army of over thirty thousand—mounted cavalry, archers, spearmen. His soldiers are... like beasts in human form. Towering, muscle-bound, drilled to breathless precision. Their shields lock together like wolf fangs. Their horses move without whisper. Their tents stretch beyond vision."
He paused, fearful of saying more.
"And their king... Alexander..." —he inhaled sharply—
"...He stands as if cast by the gods. Tall. Blonde-haired. Eyes

like burning sapphire. Unafraid. Untouched. The people cross lands only to kneel before him—not because he asks, but because they are... overcome. Even his enemies bow at his arrival. I saw kings shake before him, ministers cry merely hearing his name. His name...travels faster than his army."

A quiet shifted through the court like wind through a temple.

Purushottama remained thoughtful—more curious than afraid.

"He is no monarch we have aggrieved. No trader we've slighted. What want has he with us?"

No one answered.

Then the raja guru turned to the Greek officer again.

"Tell us... what do you know of this Alexander? Openly, and fully."

The Greek nodded solemnly.

"His name began as a prince beside his father, Philip of Macedon, who united the Greek tribes under one banner. But for Alexander... that wasn't enough. He studied under Aristotle, the greatest mind of our age, who taught him that civilization must conquer barbarism. That to be great, one must reshape the world."

He continued, his voice tightening.

"Alexander struck Egypt without a siege—he was welcomed as a god. In the city of Memphis, the priests declared him the son of Amun-Ra, the sun god himself. They adorned him with sacred emblems, offered their temples—and he accepted."

Court whispers grew quick.

"But his greatest test came in Persia, at Gaugamela, where Darius III raised an army nearly three times the size of Alexander's. Persian chariots, elephants, archers, cavalry... a sea of men. They warred from dawn to dusk. And yet..."

His voice trembled.

"Alexander outmaneuvered them. He feigned retreat, split lines, drove straight into Darius's heartline. The Great King of Persia fled. His empire crumbled. Darius was later slain

in the mountains by his own kin. And Alexander… took the empire, unbroken."
Even Purushottama, who had stared down enemies for a decade, looked down in solemn thought.
The Greek officer wasn't done.
"But conquest is not his only hunger. He is driven by legend—by the name Achilles, his hero. He believes he is destined to bridge the world. He crosses deserts, mountains, rivers… not for land, but for immortality."
"He follows his father's dream—Philip had sworn to conquer the East. Alexander carries that oath as legacy and fire. He says he will not stop 'til he reaches the edge of the world."
The court fell into awed silence.
The raja guru lowered his gaze, whispering, "Madness dressed as purpose… and yet it moves mountains."
For a long time, Purushothama sat, silent as stone. Eyes toward the distant banners of his fortress, mind weaving futures and flames.
Then he spoke.
"I have no enmity with this Alexander. I have not threatened him, nor have I shunned his caravans. We trade with his people, not his sword."
The court nodded.
"But if he wages war against those with no quarrel, then his sword is not meant to protect—but to consume."
He stood slowly from the throne.
"And yet…" he said, looking over the assembly, "who are we to offer battle without understanding his mind?"
He turned to his scribe.
"Prepare a scroll."
Pouring his resolve into words, King Purushothama dictated a letter unlike any that had crossed rivers before.
"To Alexander, King of the West,
We—the Paurava—have no cause to bear arms against you. Our rivers have not blocked your people. Our merchants

have not shorted your caravans.
If it is conquest you seek, let it be of knowledge, of connection, not flesh.
We are a proud people, living free under our skies.
You may come as a guest, and we shall drink toast at our court.
You may come as a friend, and we shall share wisdom in trade and honor.
But if you come with steel,
Know that the sun shines equally on blood from both sides of the battlefield.
And it cannot be washed from the stones so easily.
~King Purushothama of Paurava"
He sealed the scroll personally.
And turned to the messenger.
"Go. Let him hear the voice of a king before he hears the cry of my war elephants."
The court bowed as the messenger took the scroll, slipped it inside an oiled leather tube, and disappeared into the light.
Purushothama sat again.
The shadow beyond the Sindhu thickened.
And the eyes in the court no longer whispered fear—they whispered war.

Chapter 4 : No Path but Steel

The messenger set off before dawn, a retinue of porters packing the city's finest—sacks of spices bursting with scent, ivory inlaid combs, bolts of cotton, and a carved chest filled with gemstone beads—gifts meant to honor a potential trade.
Tucked within his robe, pressed to his heart with ceremonial reverence, was the letter of King Purushottama: words written in dignity, sealed in gold and indigo thread.
Crossing the river, India's scented air yielded to dust and the acrid tang of an encamped army. Far across the Sindhu, the noise and brilliance of the Greek host stretched for miles—

campfires shimmered, arms glinted like a thousand mirrors, and the drums of marching boots thudded through the earth itself. Men in bronze and horsehair helmets, with blue-painted shields and stern eyes, cut the messenger's retinue short.

He was led past lines of wagons, past throngs of spearmen and Persian mercenaries, till he reached a wide tent where gold and blood-red rugs covered the sands. There, seated on a high chair flanked by lion-motifs, was the man whose name—Alexander—had become a rumor of doom.

The Greek king regarded the messenger in silence, icy blue eyes beneath a brow furrowed in calculation. Around him, commanders wore fine wool and trophies from every land the Greeks had broken: Egypt's collars, Babylonian daggers, Scythian bracelets. The gifts were displayed with deliberate pomp, but Alexander did not reach for them.

The letter was offered first—two hands, head bowed. The silence in Alexander's tent grew cold as he read. His face flickered—first detached, then faintly insulted—before he glanced at the spices and silks, the tokens of goodwill.

He spoke in Greek, a tone mocking yet edged:

"See, my friends—these Indians send us what we perfected in Macedon and Athens. They barter as merchants with their betters, not as the vanquished should: with knees to the earth or blades drawn for the last time."

His officers laughed. Some toyed with the Indian combs, holding them up as curiosities rather than treasures.

Alexander's gaze snapped back to the messenger. Switching to the accented Aramaic the court had taught him, he asked, *"Why does your king—Puru, you call him?—resist the natural order? Has he never heard the tale of the son of Philip? Of the west, now mine, from the Aegean shore to Babylon's golden gate?"*

The messenger met his eye, trembling only slightly. "Purushottama fears not war, lord. He weighs loss and victory by the lives of his people. He has held Paurava since boyhood, bested the king of Takshashila in battle when the odds were grim. He keeps his realm whole and rich while others fracture. My king's courage and schemes are known across the Uttarapatha—he considers war only when forced, because here, it is not death we fear, but the loss of life's purpose itself."

A hush circled the tent. Alexander's mouth twisted to a smile that was nearly cruel.

"So, you uncouth tribals now send me morals? Speak of values and philosophy as if you had them first! Let me show you what becomes of your uprightness when Macedonian pikes march through Paurava." His words sharpened.

"Tell your king this: trade, talk—all worthless. There is no peace for those who will not bend. Tell him to prepare for bondage or blood. I desire nothing else now but war—and the end of his pride."

The guards signaled their dismissal. With gifts left, the messenger was led out, the Greek laughter echoing after him. He walked back through the lines—past the dusky stalls where mercenaries wagered spoils and Persian mothers wept by burnt wagons, past villages mutely emptied, small footprints in the mud where Greek horses drank, and heard the chilling tales: of towns put to the sword, markets trampled, children wailing in smoky twilight.

The return to Paurava was slower, each step burdened by memory and grief.

At the palace gate, the air was stagnant. The messenger was rushed to Purushottama's darbar; already, the council sensed the news had cracked the last hope. The king listened in grave quiet, every minister reading the weight in his set jaw. The scroll was laid bare—Alexander's reply delivered in blunt, brutal threat. The stories told by the messenger kindled low fear along the marble floors.

Silence.

At last, Purushottama stood. His eyes were narrowed, but not by uncertainty.

"So be it. When a guest refuses bread and seeks blood, hospitality dies. If Alexander wishes war, he will have it—but not unopposed. Paurava will answer steel with steel, for right is no birthright of monarchs, but of those who defend their soil with honor."

The air in the hall was taut as a drawn bow. Ministers murmured orders: the arsenal was to be readied, outlying troops recalled. The king, who had once dreamed his kingdom might weather the stranger's storm, felt a cold resolve take root.

When the court dispersed, only Raja Guru Devadatta remained. As officers and scribes withdrew, the ancient counselor approached the throne, his steps echoing wisdom and sorrow.

"War is fire that cannot choose its meal, Maharaj," the guru intoned.

"It does not spare kings or bakers, temples or sons. I had hoped this hour would never come."

Purushottama gazed at the dying light pooling beneath the palace arches. "I have known war, guru-ji. I have won by arrow and lost by trust. But never have I faced a foe who conquers only for his own name. We will need every eye open and every hand ready."

The guru nodded.

"Let me call upon our neighbors, upon those with old debts and grudging respect. And I shall send word through the Uttarapatha—our traders and spies must report every Greek breath, each hoof struck upon the road."

He paused, voice low. *"We must watch the world, for the world now watches us."*

In the dusk, Raja Guru Devadatta faded into the corridor's gloom, already marshaling his wisdom and resources in the great and silent war that must come before the swords. Alone in the throne room, Purushottama turned his eyes to the wide evening sky, uncertain whether he searched for a sign—or simply for the courage to bear what fate would next unveil.

Chapter 5: When the Kingdom Stirs

At the long table that curved like the river Vitasta, Raja Guru Devadatta laid out a scroll of sealed commands. Torches hissed behind him in the cold-shadowed chamber beneath the darbar hall. The scent of burnt oil mingled with parchment and iron dust.

King Purushottama had given the signal—no longer negotiation, but preparation. And the old sage, though he had spent half a lifetime trying to keep war at bay, now moved with the slow thunder of inevitability.

The first order: to awaken the spy network. Messengers left the palace walls at dawn, disguised as monks, caravan guides, and falcon-keepers. Their task: to blend into crowds, disappear into roads, and pierce the veil between words and warfare.

Letters, etched with invisible ink, were dispatched to informants along the Uttarapatha—from the salt stores of Mathura to the merchant houses of Varanasi. In Takshashila, spies were ordered to watch the palace of Ambhi, whose hands now cupped silver taken from the Greeks. Even within Alexander's own army, two Paurava-born translators had been awakened from slumbering ranks, their silence purchased with loyalty and oaths older than gold.

"Let us know," the raja guru had stated, voice like hammered copper, "not what the enemy says—but what he does not speak aloud."

General Veerabhalla, the lion of the southern campaigns, stepped forward next. Tall, lithe for his age, he wore the scars of decades—not just on his forearms and calloused knuckles, but in the quiet way he listened before acting. War was not rage to him—it was rhythm.

He bowed to the raja guru and the council, his fingers resting on the hilt of his side-blade.

"Ready the cavalry," the guru instructed. "Estimate the force of our swords, bows, spears, and shields. Begin drills thrice daily. Ready the chariots. Feed the elephants."
Veerabhalla bowed once again.
Legends still circled his name—of the hill revolt he crushed without spilling blood, of the border skirmish with the Malava warriors he turned with only seventy archers. He had earned not only the soldiers' respect, but their silent affection.
He mounted his horse by midday. By sunset, war-horns echoed from barracks, animal enclosures roared with motion, and the inner courtyards of Paurava echoed with the calls of bhairava warriors, mahouts, and cavalry trainers.
The city's war-arsenal, long silent, wheezed and boomed back to life like a serpent roused from rust.
Next was the Minister of Treasury, called Dhanapati Bharadwaj, whose belly was round with age but whose mind was sharper than the finest needle of Lanka's silk merchants.
Raja Guru's tone was firm.
"Stockpile gold, sharpen ledgers. We will need silver tongues to keep loyalty... and golden weights to feed the fortress, if it must breathe alone."
Dhanapati nodded once and left without comment.
Soon, the counting halls of Paurava thudded with abacus clicks. Carts of hidden bullion flickered in the early starlight as they moved to safer chambers beneath temple foundations and grain houses. Traders who had once lobbied for tax breaks now whispered offers of grain, cloth, ghee, and iron—not from patriotism, but fear.
The Guild of Cropkeepers received royal orders: triple storage in the fortress granaries. Artisans were quietly told: no luxury work now—only wheels, spears, harnesses.
The kingdom itself was not yet in battle—but it now thrummed like a bowed string.
Then began the songs of warning.

Runners, dispatchers, and herald-guards traveled the districts of the capital and nearby settlements. On the king's behalf, they proclaimed to townsfolk:

"Prepare. The kingdom faces challenge from beyond the Sindhu.

His Majesty grants rations and oil, but the hearth of war must be shared by all.

Store your grains. Bind your families. Sharpen your will."

In courtyards, messages were carved on stone. At well-markets, scrolls were nailed to the banyan trees. At temple steps, city criers raised conch and drum and spoke the king's orders aloud.

Some merchants—wealthy, fearful—packed carts that same night, heading deeper inland. Towns like Vidisha, Koshambi, or Avanti looked safer from the west wind's coming fire.

But the common folk stayed.

Weavers loomed faster under torchlight. Blacksmith fires burned past midnight. Mothers lined up at granary posts with quiet eyes. Fathers taught their sons how to string a bow again. Girls whispered omens near doorways.

Old men on thresholds remembered.

In dark corners, rumors split like storm-cracks across a brittle sky. Foreign travelers whispered of ashes left behind by Greek hooves.

Men spoke in markets:

"They say their horses wear armor like tigers."

"They stab without words. And laugh."

"A queen of Gandhara poisoned herself rather than look into their blue eyes."

From the northern hill villages, couriers brought news of Greek camps consuming wells, hill shrines burned, cattle seized.

Jewels were hidden under floorboards. Some cottages were nailed from the outside. The mighty Uttarapatha, once India's golden artery of trade, now carried fewer carts—and more rumors than goods. From traders out of Takshashila came stories of executed Brahmins, artisans pressed into slave-labor, entire temple towns plundered under the banner of Macedon.

Still, it was not merely fear that moved through the people. Among the older sages in the temples, a word returned from the oldest scrolls—a war from the prayers of rishis, the warnings of vedic chants:

Dāśarājñá Yuddhá.

The war of ten kings.

A cycle begun before. A pattern repeating through realms.

No scripture gave comfort. Only prophecy.

In steel-etched script, embossed with the royal crest, invitations were sent through torches and storms: sealed scrolls to lords of Kalinga, Malava, even distant Magadha.

Puru's words carried weight without desperation, honor without arrogance.

"A fire marches from the west.
We of Paurava stand upright, not against brothers,
But against the storm that does not ask whom it burns.
Come, gather.
Let us speak not as rivals, but as limbs of a single land."

The scrolls traveled under eagle guard, over rivers, across valleys, to palaces high and hidden.

And in the capital of Paurava, beneath banners now darkened grey, the king watched the sun fade early behind thickening clouds. Soldiers sharpened. Civilians murmured. Priests fasted.

And still no word came back from beyond the Sindhu.

Only the waiting.

Only the wind.

Chapter 6: The Calm Before the Thunder

For weeks, the horizon remained dry, but the air in Alexander's camp grew heavy—not with storm winds, but with simmering unrest.

His troops had been fighting for years. From the shores of the Aegean to the fire-tombs of Persia, through the sands of Egypt and the stones of Babylon, they had followed him—the son of Philip, the boy who never lost. But now, as they camped along the Sindhu, staring east at unknown forests and strange tongues, there was an ache that gold could not silence.

They missed home.

Far from Macedon, from wives, sons, vineyards and temples, many soldiers glanced westward and began to ask a question the king hated above all:

"Why?"

The rallies were smaller than battle cries. Quiet grumblings near fire pits. Jokes that struck too closely. Soldiers resting their heads on whetstones, not to sharpen their blades, but to dull their memories.

"I fought fifteen years," muttered one spearman, "but I've not held my daughter even once."

Another grunted: *"You can't drink glory. You can't eat history."*

A few even dared question aloud the point of chasing one more rival king into green jungles beneath the rising sun.

Alexander heard the murmurs—of course he did. His spies told him what the commanders would not. But he did not react with fury. There was no immediate execution. No whips. No shouting.

Instead, he responded with a show.

He ordered plundered treasures from nearby raids to be laid out for open claim—jewels, ornaments, carved figurines, bolts of fabric dyed in rich indigo, sandalwood, and ivory.
"Each man may take what he can carry," he said. "Claim it as your triumph."
Then came the diversions.
A wrestling ring was built within a raised enclosure of logs and vine-ropes. Participants were offered silver and wine. Alexander himself entered the ring. Lean, golden-skinned from sun and oil, draped only in a loincloth, he challenged a Thracian champion and pinned him in two turns—to thunderous applause.
Later came the exotic plays, borrowed rituals twisted to resemble both Dionysian theater and the Eastern stylings of the new land—dancers, music, foreign perfumes carried over by enslaved performers.
Wine flowed. Shields hung untouched.
Something shifted in the camp—momentary awe replacing doubt.
Then came the night.
Campfires flickered in long, jagged lines stretching to the mountain foothills. Soldiers sat in clusters, cups clinking, tongues loosened. The wrestling still lingered in laughter, but it was quiet laughter now—exhausted, unsure.
It was then, with a stone cup in hand and no crown upon his head, that Alexander stood among them.
"Do you know why I fight?" he asked, gently, a strange softness in his voice.
They quieted.
"When I was a boy, I played with wooden swords under my father's banners. The elders told me stories—of Herakles, the god-warrior, who crossed lands no mortal dared tread. I asked my tutors, 'Why not Greece?' They said Greece had always lacked one thing: a man willing to carry it over the edge of the world."
He paused, his gaze searching their eyes.

"I am that man. And if I fall short, you will still be remembered for following me."

The fire crackled louder.

He turned solemn.

"Some say we've strayed too far. Some whisper of homes and wives. I understand. But what waits in Macedon? Dust and stories. What waits here?" He pointed to the jungles beyond the river's bend. "Immortality."

Then, without warning, his tone hardened.

"And know this—those who think to oppose the star's path meet shadow. Philotas. Callisthenes. They were my blood and thought themselves wiser. One spoke too boldly. The other insulted our gods. Both rest now deep beneath Persian soil."

A chill coursed through the camp, even as the wine warmed their throats.

Then Alexander smiled, calm as dawn.

"But I offer you more. India is not one kingdom—it is many. Forests swimming in silver. Villages fat with grains. Thrones empty, waiting for a true master. You follow me—and when the blood settles, what remains will be yours."

Some men cheered. Others stared into their wine, unsure whether they had been inspired or threatened.

But rebellion died on their tongues. Whether by dream, greed, or fear, the army stood with its king again.

Meanwhile, in Paurava, the gates of the capital opened not to merchants, but monarchs.

Chariots ringed with lacquered armor rolled into the forecourt. Processions of war elephants trumpeted under well-fed flags. One by one, envoys, kings, and vassals from distant corners came—not all by loyalty, but by looming necessity.

Some came out of respect for Purushottama.

Others came out of fear of Alexander.

And a few—like Ambhi of Takshashila—came only to listen and report.

The assembly was hosted not in the inner court, but in the open pavilion—a space without walls, where the sky was listening.
Silken canopies fluttered above benches arranged in a ring. Fruit trays sat untouched. The air was too heavy for hunger. There were glances, but no greetings. Old rivalries blinked beneath smiles. Kingdoms who once vied for fertile river banks now sat side by side like strangers awaiting a common funeral.
Purushottama sat above none of them, but in their center. To his left, Raja Guru Devadatta, also silent. To his right, General Veerabhalla, dressed plain.
Whispers passed:
"Malava came late."
"Kalinga brought no war musicians—what does it mean?"
"Why is Ambhi here? Did he kiss the feet of Macedon already?"
At last, the murmur faded.
Raja Guru rose.
No flute played. No bell chimed.
He looked over the gathered kings.
"We honor the flags you carry. We grieve the trade disrupted between us. And we remember the ancestors who built these thrones by oath and blood."
He paused, as clouds gathered above in a quiet, unspoken omen.
"But we did not summon you for memory."
His next words cut across the air like chariots splitting soil.
"There is a storm coming from the west."
Silence fell like a dropped blade.

Chapter 7: Council Beneath the Gathering Clouds

The royal pavilion was shrouded in a rare hush, the air heavy with anxious expectation and scented by marigold garlands. Courtiers and guards pressed to the walls, their gazes flickering between veiled tensions and the rising orchestra of distant drums. The banners of myriad kingdoms—each marked with animals, mountains, or rivers—fluttered around the circle of assembled rulers, reflecting both the old rivalries and the faint hope of unity.

At the head of the dais, Raja Guru Devadatta rose, his presence calming as monsoon mist before thunder. His voice, neither urgent nor resigned, carried clear to every corner.

"A storm from the west approaches. This, you all know—not from a single tongue, but from the whispers that have crossed your courts, through hidden letters and returning spies. The name at the heart of this storm is Alexander."

Murmurs swept the circle. Some kings looked elsewhere, weighing their own calculations. For centuries, the land of Bharat had known threats from the north, the hills, the steppe. But never from a world beyond their maps.

The Raja Guru paused, letting the moment settle before continuing.

"Why would anyone come so far, bearing arms against our soil, crossing deserts and kingdoms not their own? Many of you hope—honorably—that the lands beyond will blunt this storm, that these invaders will waste themselves before they ever reach your frontiers. Others here see the merit in caution, for you are not moved by selfishness, but by a king's duty to shield his people from war if it can be avoided."

Heads nodded in the assembly. A few eyes darted toward their own generals and envoys, seeking counsel in silence.

"And yet," the Raja Guru intoned, drawing scrolls from his cloak, "we have proof: Alexander's intentions are clear.

Here are messages he himself has sent—not just to Paurava, but to others in these very lands. His letters speak not of trade, nor of peaceful passage, but of conquest, glory, and the desire to see all the world kneel beneath his banner."

He held up the scroll, the foreign sigil stark against the parchment.

"He comes not as guest, but as kingmaker—and kingslayer. Alone, each of us will face his wrath when our turn arrives. Together, our strengths would be tenfold, and the storm might break on our united shield, with minimal loss to men and wealth."

It was a direct call for unity—one that echoed above the doubts, the personal fears, and ambitions that clung to the gathering.

For a moment, the council was silent. Then, the first to speak was Dhananda, king of Magadha—the richest and mightiest in the Ganga plains. His voice was calm, lined with both assurance and calculated distance.

"My lands lie deep in the heart of Bharat. Our fortresses and armies are vast, and any who outlast these border storms must still breach Magadha's gates. We do not face an immediate threat. But on the ground of dharma, I will provide: armories and granaries for your civilians—let your non-combatants and wounded find safety with us. But my legions will stay in Magadha, until their need is certain."

The council rippled with surprise and mild disappointment. Out of the silence, Ambhi of Takshashila—the notorious adversary of Purushottama—stood up. His reputation for cunning was only exceeded by his ability to choose sides. But his announcement stunned even the skeptics.

"I set aside our past enmity, King Puru. I will send my troops to aid your cause. If the storm topples you, we will all be swept into the flood. Let us stand as one, for now."

An uneasy hush fell, broken only by Purushottama himself. Rising with restrained grace, he inclined his head toward Ambhi, voice free of bitterness.

"If an old enemy has found new wisdom, let the past remain as lesson, not as shackle. Your courage today will be our shield tomorrow."

Moments later, the Malava king, burdened by old wars, joined in, albeit cautiously.

"You have my finest war elephants and the best horses from our grasslands. But I cannot spare men from my borders—they are stretched even now."

Assent murmured from a few tribal chieftains and minor rulers, many of whom had seen firsthand what Alexander's men left behind: blackened fields, ruined villages, families scattered like chaff. One by one, they pledged their archers, scouts, or jungle warriors—rough voices bridging ancient divides.

But not all voices spoke. Several kings chose silence over commitment, studying their polished fingernails, pensively tracing the runes on their armrests. Their loyalties were unclear—perhaps hoping to bide their time, or gambling that Alexander's wrath would pass them by.

Purushottama noted it all, his face an unreadable mask. He responded without a trace of rancor.

"May the gods bless whatever you choose to offer: be it grain, arms, warriors, or only fair wishes. Even if I must stand alone, I will hold the flood at our motherland's frontier. If I fall, may the rest of Bharat rise higher still. Let this day, if nothing else, bind us to duty, not fear."

With that, he gestured for the scribes to draw up mutual bonds and seals—a gesture less of triumph than of necessity. The court echoed with the scratching of reeds on palm leaves, clay pressed into wax seals, hurried signatures.

When the council dissolved, a complicated mood swept through the capital. In the streets and bazaar squares, people gawked at the procession of chariots and banners, the spectacle of rival kings walking as one—if only briefly. To some, it became a source of unexpected hope:

“ *Every throne in Bharat stands with Paurava—surely, the storm will break and pass* .” To others, the sight created new worries:
“ *If these great ones quarrel, will they tear this city apart among themselves?* ”
Whispers of old betrayals haunted even the most festive corners.
Among all these, it was the common folk—the artisans, merchants, mothers and elders—who read the omens with the most clarity. They listened to the wind and remembered stories of invasion, of alliances made and broken. Some prayed for unity; others simply prayed for mercy. All waited for the first thunder of horse-hooves or the next message on the wind—uncertain if it would signal deliverance or destruction.
As the council ended, and the kings, lords, and tribal chieftains mounted their carriages to return to their scattered realms, the sky outside gathered weight and darkness. Across Paurava, hope mingled with dread: history itself was poised, sharp-edged and breathless, awaiting the first drop of rain.

Chapter 8: March of the Thunder

For a month they waited.
The Macedonian army had encamped leagues away from the Hydaspes, deep enough into the foreign land to sense its pulse, yet far enough to cast no shadow across the river’s edge. There, in the folds between unfamiliar hills and fractured jungle paths, Alexander’s men plundered the villages—stripping gold, seizing grain and livestock, and carving a path into lands that hadn’t yet resisted.
The waiting was not due to hesitation; it was design. Alexander preferred not to strike immediately. He wanted the air of caution to mask aggression—wanted his name to echo before his army ever arrived.

"Let them know I'm coming," he had said to his generals, as his banner was raised above a desecrated hill shrine. "But not when."

And now, at last, the wait was over.

He summoned his commanders at dawn. Light filtered through the gauze canopy of his war tent. Oil lamps were dimmed. Scrolls of terrain maps lay stretched across stone tables.

One by one, the generals entered—Hephaestion, Ptolemy, Seleucus, Perdiccas—men hardened by the deserts of Egypt and the fires of Gaugamela. Behind them, scribes crowded with tablets, while war engineers stood poised for instruction.

"We move east," Alexander said, straightening his tunic strap. "The Hydaspes has waited long enough."

Orders crackled through the ranks like lightning striking dry grass. Horns blew. Infantry captains assembled their men. Messengers galloped from sector to sector, banner-sashes tied to their backs to distinguish company lines.

The camp came alive.

Tents were brought down in rows, their silk and hide rolled tight. Cartwrights reinforced pallets, wheels bound in leather to cushion for rain-slick plains.

Soldiers loaded what remained of their loot—grain sacks, wine jars, captured gold—into caravans pulled by bullocks and elephants.

Senior officers were given palanquins, iron-framed and cloth-covered, to protect them from the sweltering heat and insects. Beasts of burden were aligned by weight class. The armory was polished, packed, and placed on central wagons, guarded on all sides.

In the midst of all this, the Greek command reassembled to plan the locomotion of thirty thousand men.

"Divided, we fall," Hephaestion reminded the tent.

"So we march like a spine," Alexander said. "No gaps. No flanks exposed."

The cavalry was organized into four divisions:

The vanguard, fastest and strongest, would lead the approach and cut scouting paths.

The rear guard would carry engineers and craftsmen, responsible for field repairs.

The left and right flanks were shields—well-armored cavalry with archer units embedded.

One hundred elite riders, Macedonian-born and trained in both sword and bow, were dispatched as advance scouts—to ride ahead and observe the road, the river, and the silence between.

For seven days, the army prepared. For seven nights, dancers were dismissed, wine was rationed, and Alexander walked the campfires like a ghost of iron. He did not speak much. He only inspected. War was close now, and the theatre was unmoving.

On the morning of the eighth day, a silence fell like prophecy.

And then came the command.

Alexander mounted Bucephalus, the great war horse of thunder-black coat and fire-tipped mane—the beast said to know battle better than mapmakers knew borders. The generals rode beside him.

The army began to move.

The earth trembled beneath their feet. Thousands of boots marched in rhythm. Shields clanged against thighs, spears glinted beneath slow-rising sun. A dust cloud rose, thick and wide and endless, as if even the ground tried to resist the feet that would crush it.

The Macedonian war machine moved like a city on the march—calculated, unstoppable, deliberate.

Above the horizon, it looked like a sandstorm in an Arabian desert, rolling inward.

On the eastern ridges, a man crouched in the trees.

Wrapped in grey-black robes of mountain dye, his face smeared in ash and bark oil, the Paurava spy watched the dust rise. The sound came first—low thunder, not of rain, but of trampling beasts and synchronized war drums.

He whispered a chant to himself, kissed a cloth tied to his wrist, and turned.

His message was already written. The scroll tucked into an oilskin wrap beneath his vest bore only one sentence:

"The march has begun."

By nightfall, the message crossed the river.

By morning, it reached Purushottama's palace.

In Paurava, the streets tightened. Saris were drawn back, lips whispered behind latticed windows. Temple bells rang twice the usual count, and priests burned sandalwood in every shrine. Children were pulled indoors. Weapon forges screamed like iron childbirth.

The war was no longer coming. It had arrived.

The court moved swiftly. Barracks were expanded. Grain was weighed and sealed. Palisade spikes were tested for brittleness. Purushottama summoned his war council.

The throne room, once rich with trade maps and festival scrolls, now bore only a table of formation plans. The Raja Guru stood beside the king. Elephants in battle gear practiced outside, shaking the courtyards with their footfalls.

"They march in formation," Purushottama said calmly. "Which means they believe the frontier will not waver."

The raja guru nodded. "Then it must."

Not with chaos, but with resistance.

Across the river, Alexander came—wind behind him, gods conjured above him, the cries of conquered cities echoing like songs.

But so did Puru.

With towers that stood longer than memory, hands curled around swords trained by Dharma and dust, minds steeled not for glory—but for survival.

And the river waited.

Chapter 9: The Blood That Moves a Mountain

The moment the message arrived, Purushottama was already on his feet.

"They march," the courier whispered, his robe soaked in sweat and river mist. "The dust rises behind them like fire smoke. They do not rest."

In the eastern court, the air shifted. Temple bells began to ring longer, and the chants of the priests echoed louder than before. Preparation now had a pulse.

Purushottama did not retreat to his throne. That same midday, he left the palace armory in plain attire—no crown, no diamonds, no ornaments—and entered the central training camp. There, among hundreds of soldiers, he stood barehanded and nodded once.

"Today, I will train with you," he said.

He took up a spear.

His movements began slowly—controlled arcs, leg pivoting, weight evenly distributed. The soldiers held their breath. Some bowed. Others forgot their stances.

Then Puru quickened. Spears clashed. The king spun, feinted, drove the shaft with such precision that the training master involuntarily stepped back—twice. The camp roared.

Later that day, he rotated among the ranks—mud-wrestling pits, sword duels, bare-hand grapples. Not as a spectator, but a challenger.

His message was clear: *"I do not ask of you what I will not face myself."*

Morale surged. A living legend was now one of them.

At the south enclosure, the war elephants were restless. These massive beasts, so often gods in motion, had known ceremonial parades—but Puru had different plans.

"They must learn the sound of dying men," he told Veerabhalla, "and not flinch when the air burns."

Torches were lit. Cymbals clashed beside them. Whips cracked—not in pain, but rhythm. Water was thrown. Metal drums rolled. The elephants reared and trumpeted—but gradually, by second dusk, they stood firm.

Tusk armor was tightened. Mahouts were instructed to strike once, retreat, strike again. Arrows dipped in fire were shot past them to steel their nerves.

At the cavalry yards, Puru reviewed horse troops and pointed out flaws in mounting posture, advising riders to loosen the knee just before an uphill rush. He had learned from seasoned riders of the Vindhya passages during his youth—and now he used that knowledge to perfect his army spine.

He moved to the archery fields.

"Don't pull the string. Whisper it," he told a young archer. He loosed three arrows himself, each hitting within the same palm-width circle.

Despite the growing shadow, Puru walked the marketplace, treating it as battlefield and sacred zone both.

Merchants greeted him with tight fists. The once-booming stalls had fallen into murmurs. Salt, oil, and ghee were sold in whispers rather than calls. Children clung to mothers. Couriers wove between carts like shadows.

But when the king appeared, everything paused.

Puru pointed at the silk bales still unpacked. *"Sell your colors,"* he said. " *Even war deserves beauty."*

He handed a child a fresh roll of honeyed rice. He turned to the people and spoke:

"We do not wait for the winds to choose us. We shape them with our breath. I do not rule over animals to be offered—I hold warriors, craftsmen, farmers, mothers, blood bound not by coin, but cause. If the storm reaches our gates, it will learn we were already thundering."

That night, markets began to stir again. Traders reopened chests. Fragrance returned to the air.

Hope was kindled—not by gold, but by leadership seen, not heard.

Back in the palace, departments convened one by one. Dhanapati Bharadwaj reported on granary gates. Raja Guru brought updates from weather readers. Steel-smiths submitted spear counts with pride.

Puru stood at his map chamber longer than usual, scanning distances, terrain markings, water points, and the islands that dotted the Hydaspes.

He did not speak.

But in his mind, formations formed—where the archers would stand, where the elephants must break formation, where the hidden arrow carts could be placed along ridges.

That is when the tribal chieftains arrived.

The hall reeked of neem oil, tamarind, and the guttural chants of the forest tongue. These chiefs were not polished kings but wary-eyed survivalists. Skins draped over shoulders, feather ornaments tucked behind ears, bamboo knives resting on hips.

Puru greeted them with palms pressed and a warrior's gaze.

"The enemy walks in tight columns. What they know in plains makes them blind in trees."

The chieftains agreed. Some promised their guerrilla warriors would train Paurava soldiers in:

- Camouflage, movement without sound
- Ambush tactics
- Use of natural noise to misdirect cavalry

Others—masters of herbs and poisons—offered more.

"This root here," one said, showing a dark tendril in water, "numbs faster than cold. Apply it to arrow tips."

They created poisoned darts, anointed small blades.

One tribe, keepers of sentient monkeys trained for foraging and mimicry, offered something strange. A demonstration followed: with hand signals and meat-sharing gestures, a single elder commanded five monkeys to retrieve wooden tokens from hidden corners across the garden.

Puru smiled.

"In war, even the forest grows teeth."

The tribal warriors were not treated as scouts. Puru gave many of them command stripes, placing them as advisors to the generals. The army grew not just in size, but in vision.
The spy network, long nurtured by the Raja Guru, now moved like lightning across borders. Signals came by smoke in hilltops, eagle flights, hidden ink beneath merchant scrolls.
Every movement of Alexander's force—how many days they rested, what symbolism flew on their banners, how many horses per water break—was recorded.
And then came the final signal:
"They've reached the river."
From the highest eastern ridge, flanking the Hydaspes, black flags rose—Alexander's army had arrived.
On the western bank, a forest of tents emerged. Campfires glowed against iron skin. The rumble of wooden construction echoed—siege platforms, horse pens, barriers.
The winds from the west blew stronger, stifling the incense trails of eastern temples.
The river, silent for centuries, now reflected two skies: one *gold with morning hope* , and the other *charcoal with oncoming fate* .
It had been nearly two millennia since the waters last bore witness to kings devouring kings.
It would soon happen again.

Chapter 10: In the Forest of Shadows

The Hydaspes had no voice, but it trembled.
Dense jungles rimmed the west bank, alive with humidity, buzz, and the eerie rustle of monsoon-soaked leaves.
Alexander's army—worn by sand from Persia, sun from Egypt, and blood from countless sieges—now stood beneath a canopy that whispered danger.

The men called it a green trap, a fortress shaped by gods, not mortals.

And yet, Alexander had arrived not to marvel at India. He had come to claim it.

Instead of an open battlefield, Alexander found trees growing thick as defenders and trails too narrow for phalanxes. So he carved his own path.

For ten days, steel and sweat cleared vast swaths of land. Those who carried axes worked from dawn to dusk, cutting a plain where no plain had existed—a heart of order embedded in the chaos of jungle.

> The main camp—for Alexander, Hephaestion, Seleucus, and high command—was constructed on elevated ground near a sharp curve of the river.
>
> The forest around them was left dense, but networks of hidden camps and concealed watch posts were installed every few hundred yards. These acted as traps, checkpoints, or resting zones.
>
> High timber towers were erected, visible only from inside the main camp. These stood as lookout posts, relaying light signals to track night movement.
>
> Carpets, silks, and polished wooden floors were laid in the royal quarters—a stark, unsettling contrast to the trunks and thorns just footsteps away.

"Let the jungle think we fear it," Alexander remarked, surveying the camp by night, "and then watch as we twist it to our purpose."

Here in the realm of beasts and monsoon gods, he established a city of war.

The forest could not simply be studied—it had to be learned. Alexander sent out three separate units, 300–400 men each, to sweep in different directions:

> One cohort moved north along the riverside, escorting mapmakers and supply scavengers.
>
> A second group was sent deep into the marsh zones looking to find terrain suited for surprise crossings.

The third roamed southward following scout reports of scattered forest tribes.

Their orders were blunt:

"Find the land's bones. And take its pulse from the people."

The three groups moved as instructed—but what they found was not nothing.

They crossed paths with various forest tribes—some farmers, some warrior bands, others small communities of bead-workers and jungle guides. Some greeted the soldiers with offerings, beads, or calls for peace, seeking mercy.

None were shown any.

Alexander had seen what mercy brought in Bactria.

Resistance was born from mercy. So this time, he let blood speak.

Greek captains were ordered to

"cut down the hands before the arms rise." Chiefs were singled out—leaders, priests, and battle-seasoned elders were publicly executed. Bodies were hanged in rows along the forest's midway clearings.

Those who knelt were allowed to live—but only as informants or hostages.

Across the three missions, Greek troops captured around 200 locals, including families, guides, and craftsmen. Roughly eighty of these men were executed within days—primarily those who had resisted or shown signs of loyalty to Purushottama.

Those who remained were broken piece by piece.

One was forced to watch his son's fingers crushed beneath an iron cylinder unless he drew a map of hidden jungle paths.

Another, a chieftain woman, was told her daughter would be sold into sexual slavery unless she trained Greek scouts on where elephants might hide in flooded terrain.

Faced with horror, truth spilled from many mouths.

What they gave Alexander was more than terrain. It was intelligence.

From their stories came details of temple networks, known pavilions, family safehouses. They described how Paurava used birds and smoke signals, how soldiers disguised themselves with jungle paint. They told of sentry tunnels and camouflaged trenches, and the *belief* that the jungle itself protected Puru.

Alexander listened.

That night, he ordered a new sweep.

Within 48 hours, his Greek informers uncovered and killed nearly fifty spies hiding within the army camp—many disguised as cooks, porters, even musicians. Some were beheaded. Others died screaming under Greek interrogation—long before their messages ever reached Puru.

"This," Alexander said grimly to Hephaestion, "is the first wound I deal to my enemy. Sight."

And he added:

"These forests shall hear the war cry in our tongue, and know who their new gods are."

The camp, brutal as it was, eventually stabilized. Soldiers grew accustomed to the insect buzz. Elephants loomed in dreams. Fires burned slower, thicker. But restlessness remained—heat, enemy proximity, the River that never slept.

On the twelfth night, a rider emerged with a scroll bearing an emerald seal—the mark of Ambhi, King of Takshashila.

He rode to the outer checkpoint flying a neutral flag, draped in ceremonial white. Aides led him through a checkpoint maze, passed war dogs and archers, to the main pavilion where Alexander feasted quietly with his high command.

The scroll was laid beside a roasted boar, blood still steaming at the base.

Alexander opened it and glanced once.

Silence fell over the tent.

The words were plainly written but seeded with double meaning—Ambhi requested a private meeting, outside formal witness, to "discuss further dedication of cooperation in defense of the true order of the land."

Seleucus leaned forward.
"It could be a play."
Hephaestion bristled.
"He sees which way the wind turns. Perhaps he wants to betray Puru when the swords rise."
But Alexander's expression hardened—not angered, not intrigued, but ancient.
"If he's a sheep," he said, standing, "we'll use him and then skin him."
"If he's a fox, we catch him by the neck and mark him with a lesson for every other prince of India who thinks dishonor stands."
"Either way—we kill. And use."
He folded the scroll, nodded to his scribe to prepare a return signal, and turned to the map.
Outside, the wind changed.
From the west, it came cold now.
The jungle fell silent.
The Hydaspes, ancient, restless, and infinite, waited again—its waters had run still too long.
And both kings now stood on its edge.

Chapter 11: A Fox Among Gods

The scroll bore no fanfare, only a soft green seal and the scent of folded deception.
"Come alone," it read, "unarmed. I, King Ambhi of Takshashila, will do the same. Let us speak—one king to another—where forest shadows guard what men must not hear."
Alexander read the message once more beneath the torchlight, thumb grazing the delicate fibers of the parchment.

"He invites me to meet as shadows do," he whispered. "Then let him find a shadow."
Hephaestion objected first. "A trap."
Seleucus said simply, "No king calls another into darkness unless he brings teeth with him."
Alexander nodded. "Which is why I will go."
Before either could protest, he raised a hand.
"Station fifty men where the bamboo sways loudest. Hidden, unseen—within reach of my signal, but beneath my silence. If he comes with swords, they meet Greek steel in two breaths. But if he brings lies... let us see if I still remember how to deal with those."
And with nothing more than a simple cloak over his shoulders, Alexander rode into the trees.
It was nearly half an hour's walk from the main clearing where the scouts had prepared the path—through thickets strung with roots and knotted vines, where the trees separated not to welcome him, but as if afraid.
A ringed grove had been prepared—hollow and silent, with dry leaves crackling underfoot and no bird in the sky.
Alexander arrived first.
He stepped alone, unarmed, barefoot on sacred soil. Just as instructed.
The river hummed somewhere behind him, torches flickered faintly in the outer forest. Stillness reigned. Moments passed. Ten. Fifteen. Twenty.
Then something changed.
Not in sound—but in instinct, in that warrior's gland that never sleeps behind the ribs.
Alexander's left foot curled slightly. His knees bent.
"So," he murmured, "Ambhi the fox wears sheep's fur after all."
A smirk broke across his face. The kind that had drained kings of their certainty, the kind painted in battlefield tapestries from Thebes to Tyre.

He saw no one. But he felt it—the ripple of muscle above him.

Then the trees came alive.

Ten men dropped from the canopy like warped birds of prey—cloaked in dark hide and armed with axes, sickles, barbs, and curved tribal swords. Their bodies were wiry, limbs long, pressure in their knees poised to explode.

No introduction. No demand.

Just death in motion.

They surged forward—ten predators striking the one man they believed alone.

Alexander did not backpedal. He did not call for help.

He leapt.

One axe passed where his shoulder had just been.

He twisted mid-air, pushed off a tree trunk with his bare foot, flipped behind one attacker, and slammed a palm into the man's throat—crushing his windpipe like bark.

The man gasped once, vomited blood, and collapsed in the leaves.

Two more charged. One swung wide but too slow. The other aimed for Alexander's head with a sickle.

The king ducked, spun low like a panther, grabbed the attacker's ankles mid-motion, and swept him clean off the ground.

Another slash nicked his cloak. He tore it off.

Now half-naked, skin gleaming with sweat, the Macedonian warrior advanced without fear—without hesitation—without mercy.

The fifth man struck high. Alexander caught the wrist, yanked the arm down, and twisted—

CRACK.

The bone snapped like dry parchment. The scream was brief.

Alexander seized the attacker's fallen axe, turned, and buried the blade deep into the seventh man's throat.

The body separated before it hit the ground.

Now there were three left.

They circled, horrified. This was no king. This was Herakles reborn. Muscle did not move like this unless it was bred on Olympus.

Alexander rushed like a storm before strategy could return to their limbs. The axe whispered through the humid air, cutting territory over throats and stomachs alike.

The forest was now stained.

Crimson pooled between wooden roots, flies gathering mid-fight. The final man tried to run—

The axe caught wind—and then spine.

Silence returned.

Alexander stood, glistening like a bloodied statue, breathing low and sharp through his teeth. His arms drooped. The axe's handle steamed. His shoulder bore a shallow nick, but nothing more.

He was stained head to ankle in the blood of ten men.

And he was grinning.

From the path behind him, a figure appeared, walking softly.

A white robe swayed above beaded sandals.

Ambhi.

The King of Takshashila stepped into the ring, stopping where limbs lay warm on the grass.

A Greek translator followed, nervous, eyes darting.

His expression read panic.

Ambhi motioned toward the blood.

"I see your stories are not exaggerated."

Alexander's response was stillness. His chest rising. His eyes terrifyingly calm.

"This hunt had better come with worth," he murmured, blood dripping from his fingertips. "Or I will paint a second ring with your body."

Ambhi didn't flinch.

"These were not my men. They were loyalists of Purushottama. I intercepted word of the trap. And I chose not to stop it."

He paused, smiled faintly.

"Instead, I watched."

The words were soft—measured. The translator stumbled over them in Greek, but when Alexander understood, his brows raised slightly.

Ambhi continued.

"Puru is strong. Too strong. I feared his cause. I promised him support only to avoid his suspicion. But in war, I must survive. And in order to betray the king, I first needed to see the man I would offer my loyalty to instead."

Alexander looked him over now, truly. Ambhi, taller than average but built like a merchant turned prince, not tempered by years of swordcraft. No battle marks. But he stood straight.

His hands did not shake.

His eyes?

Poison.

The kind you didn't taste until too late.

"You watched me fight for your loyalty?" Alexander asked.

"No. I watched you kill gods with your hands."

A pause.

Then came the offer.

"I will honor my promise to Puru. I will send my regiment north when war horns sound."

Alexander's mouth twitched, baffled.

"To him?"

Ambhi's voice darkened.

"But not before the horns fade. When you and he are already aligned for battle, I will send only a handful of archers. Enough that even village children will mock it."

He stepped closer.

"Then, after you win, I will send you the rest. My army, the city, its gold, and full tribute. Make me your vassal. I wear no crown that stands alone. Not anymore."

Alexander looked at this man—not tall, not fearsome, but coiled like a striking serpent—and for the briefest instant, he felt disgust.

"You betray your brother."
"Better to survive in servitude than burn in honor."
Alexander took a breath and flicked the blood from his fingers.
"You will help me. And I will let you live. But sheep who wear fox fur run one risk."
"What is that?"
"They never quite stop smelling like wolves."
Ambhi nodded, bowed slightly.
And when he vanished back into the jungle, the Greek translator remained frozen. His knees trembled. He could not speak.
Alexander walked past him, threw the bloodied axe into a puddle, and whispered:
"Even rivers will mourn this war."
And far behind him, the waters of Hydaspes lapped the earth like a weeping child.
For the river knew…
Even truth had drowned before the first sword was drawn.

Chapter 12: Shadows Beneath the Banyan

The forest held secrets as ancient as the land itself—a language woven in rustling leaves, whispered winds, and eyes unseen to the untrained gaze.
Amid the dense canopy of towering banyans and shimmying tamarisks, sleek and nimble shadows flitted.
They were not spirits, as old wives might say, but troops of a different kind: monkeys, trained by tribal allies of Paurava to serve as the kingdom's eyes and ears in the jungle's dense currency of sound and motion.
They moved silently, weaving between branches and darting from tree to tree, trained to watch and return swiftly with signs and subtle signals. Humans, especially enemy spies,

might see a blur or hear a rustle and dismiss it as forest life—but the tribal warriors knew the language of these creatures keen as any code, reading their calls and gestures as vividly as scrolls in the royal library.

When Alexander unleashed his three scouting troops into the colored labyrinth of the monsoon forests—ferocious, impenetrable, humming with unseen dangers—the tribes paid a bloody price. Fierce skirmishes echoed through the woods. Arrows blackened the sky; cries broke the heavy air. Tribal leaders fell to steel and fire, blood soaking the ancient soil like ink on a page.

Some warriors perished in the fight; others, caught and trembling, were dragged away as prisoners, their pleas muffled beneath cruel threats for their kin's lives. Yet all the while, the monkeys watched and remembered.

Then came the encounter—the ambush on Alexander himself, the furious, barehanded battle fought in the shadow of the ancient trees, the ten attackers swiftly felled by the godlike Macedonian king.

Through their bustling gestures and urgent calls, the monkeys conveyed the extraordinary tale to their handlers—experienced tribal scouts who, with practiced eyes and ears, understood the gravity of what the creatures reported.

News of the secret parley between Ambhi and Alexander soon rippled through the forest, carried invisibly yet unerringly by the small army of silent messengers. Though the monkeys could not comprehend words, the stark tableau—the fierce combat, the unexpected meeting—was clear to those trained to read the wild's language.

The message did not take long to reach the heart of Paurava. At the palace's sanctum, where sandalwood incense filled the air with calm urgency, Purushottama sat poised on a low dais, his gaze steady as the folded scroll lay before him. Beside him, Raja Guru Devadatta lowered his eyes in contemplation.

"So the shadow we feared has stepped fully into the light," spoke the Raja Guru with measured sorrow. *"Ambhi, veiled in friendship, bears the serpent's bite."*

Purushottama exhaled slowly, the weight of shattered trust pressing down. "It was not a question of if, but when," he said, serenity colored with disappointment. *"Yet to behold its truth strikes all the same."*

Their eyes met, sharing the quiet burden of leadership—knowing a direct assault on Ambhi now might dismantle fragile alliances and unravel the strength needed against the greater enemy.

"We parry in silence," uttered the Raja Guru, "but prepare to strike without hesitation."

The king rose, summoning Veerabhalla, the sentinel of Paurava's shield.

When the commander entered, bowed, and listened, Purushottama's voice was firm.

"Veerabhalla, the dagger is already among our closest. Ambhi's spies walk as merchants and mendicants. Their shadow crosses our temples and markets. Root them from the light."

Veerabhalla's gaze sharpened. *"My hand will be swift, my eyes unseen. I shall raise a band of hunters cloaked as commoners. Their blood and silence shall guard the city."*

Thus was born Paurava's silent battalion, ghostlike protectors haunting urban streets and sacred alleys alike. Their weapons light, their intent deadly, they wove through the city's lifeblood—watchful, vigilant, ready to extinguish treachery as swiftly as it flared.

Meanwhile, reports from scouts and tribal messengers illuminated the fate of the larger war. Each intercepted whisper, each hidden correspondence was scrutinized in the courts of silence where Purushottama and Rajaguru conferred—defining the chessboard of looming conflict between cunning and honor.

True to word, the promises sworn at the council bore fruit as allies delivered elephants, horses, and grain to Paurava's gates. Though far from an army united, these were threads in a tapestry hoping to become unbreakable.

Across the darkened river, Alexander's camp nestled against the jungle's edge—a sprawling blend of order and untamed wilderness. The great Macedonian host, weary but resolute, adapted to the treacherous rains, the unfamiliar calls of birds and beasts, the thickening earth under heavy monsoon skies. It was here, amid whispered winds and solemn war drums, that Alexander received another scroll bearing the seal of Ambhi—a summons veiled in cautious alliance yet ripe with hidden meaning.

Before torchlight, Alexander's eyes glinted with unyielding will as the scroll was read, foreshadowing the deadly dance yet to unfold—a dance where trust was a blade sharper than any sword.

Back in Paurava, the flicker of flame danced against the carved pillars. Purushottama's eyes, unwavering, traced the shadows lengthening across the stone floor. He felt the weight of unseen enemies—the whispered web of Ambhi's duplicity and Alexander's relentless gaze.

The river flowed beneath, ancient witness to kings, traitors, and the tempest that would decide a nation's fate.

Chapter 13: Among Shadows and Swords

The city of Paurava shimmered with an anxious energy, tense as a drawn bowstring. Soldiers disguised as merchants, traders, and artisans filtered through the crowded squares, their eyes alert behind friendly masks. Veerabhalla's elite had blended into the city's daily life, watching for threats that might move in a whisper or in plain sight.

Across the market lanes, the ordinary struggles of war played out. A middle-aged silk trader, once proud of his glimmering wares, now offered them at near loss, muttering under his breath, *"Any coin is better than empty hands."* Luxuries—gems, perfumes, exotic food—sat largely untouched, while the price of lentils soared and even plain grain was hoarded without regret. Despite rising costs, people paid, the urge for safety overtaking any other bargain.

In the hazy afternoon, a beggar settled in the city's heart. His torn cloak did little to hide the sheen of imported silk—far too fine for a vagrant. One undercover soldier caught the incongruity, shadowing the beggar's path as he drifted between almsgivers and city guards.

Elsewhere, near a weapons stall, a supposed trader drew appreciative murmurs for his show of a finely balanced sword. He swung the blade not as a merchant, but with the smooth violence of one who'd used such a sword in war. An observing spy took note, following him as dusk deepened.

Night fell, and with it came the hour of secrets.

Near the crumbling edge of the old city wall, the beggar and weapon trader met another, exchanging signals before ducking into a half-ruined alley. The elite soldiers closed in, shadows converging—a brief, brutal clash echoed in the darkness. One alleged spy managed to escape, limping and bloodied into the maze of alleys, but two others were subdued. As they were dragged toward the palace, one bit hard on something hidden, dying swiftly—the bitter tang of poison on his tongue. The second tried and failed, pinned and bound by the soldiers who hustled him to the prison for questioning.

The interrogation was ugly and raw. Under torchlight, two guards demanded names, plans, accomplices. The spy remained silent until pain broke his will. Gasping, he let slip: *"There will be an attack on your people—civilians—"* His voice faltered, and just as his eyes darted toward one of the soldiers, that guard twisted sharply, breaking his neck with practiced violence.

The chamber fell silent, shocked by the suddenness. The killer-guard looked pale beneath the blood, muttering, " *He struggled... it happened fast.*" But the other interrogator's eyes narrowed a fraction, the air thick with suspicion.

At dawn, Veerabhalla and the remaining guards reported to the palace. King Purushottama sat at a scroll-laden table, jaw set. Beside him, Raja Guru Devadatta watched each man with keen, unwavering eyes.

"He said there'd be an attack—on our own people," the guard relayed, voice low.

The Raja Guru pressed, *"Did he say when, or how?"*

The men shook their heads. "He died before he could finish. It was sudden."

But as Purushottama's gaze lingered on the captain who brought the news, he noticed a flicker too quickly—a touch of discomfort, averted eyes. He did not speak of it openly, choosing instead to focus on the immediate threat.

" *Station more warriors as merchants and masons* ," Purushottama instructed. *"No gate is safe, no alley clean, until this menace is ended. Let the spy who escaped know: he is being hunted, not hidden."*

Later, privately, the Raja Guru voiced his misgivings. " *There are wolves among your hounds, Maharaj. We do not know the true message we lost tonight."*

Purushottama's response was grim but determined: *"Until battle lines are drawn on earth, they are drawn in shadow."*

Beyond the city, the cloud of war thickened. But within Paurava's walls, the sense grew—not just of armies waiting, but of loyalty and betrayal moving in the spaces between.

Chapter 14: The Night Before No Moon

The Hydaspes flowed, swollen by the last storms of the season. Upon its banks, both east and west, torches flickered and shadows plotted.

Within a curtained tent, beneath the restless drone of night insects, Alexander gazed over his maps. Before him lay Ambhi, King of Taxila—face drawn, eyes glinting with ambition and unease. Outside the thin canvas door, two guards whispered in Greek; inside, strategies tumbled forth like dice.

Ambhi broke the silence. "Your men tire, Alexander. The fevers have taken more than battle these weeks. You have genius and strength—let me be your eyes while your army rests."

Alexander's jaw worked behind a simmering smile. "And in return, I remain your shield against Puru—so long as you remember which side of the sword cuts."

Ambhi nodded. Their pact had moved beyond words now; it pulsed with coded scrolls, with shipments of healing herbs and spices from Taxila to the sickly Macedonian ranks. Even so, both men met with wariness—each weighing the price and profit of betrayal as only kings can.

Information flowed freely between them:

> Reports of troop sicknesses.The names of city officials and traders wavering in loyalty.The vulnerabilities of Paurava's markets and the feast days when the city's defenses thinned.

More than once, Alexander reminded himself: *A fox is never tamed, only sharpened.*

When the complaints among his soldiers swelled again—grumbling to go home, ready to mutiny over river-fever and unseen enemies—Alexander hardened his resolve. This campaign must end soon. Victory must come. If he could not give them spoils, he would give them violence.

So, in the darkest watch of night, Ambhi and Alexander mapped the shape of chaos:

"We strike from within," Ambhi said, voice level. "I have men inside Paurava: tradesmen, healers, even two among Puru's own quartermasters. With your support—your soldiers disguised as foreign traders, each branded with my merchant seal—we seed the city, wait, and strike at its heart ."

Alexander arched his brow. "On what night?"

"Amāvasyā." The new moon, when gloom is deepest and lamps burn only for the lost. *"Let the gods veil your swords. My spies will kill selected commanders, moneylenders, and the grain traders—the worm at the root. Some civilians, too, to fan panic: it must feel random, not planned. Your men will ignite the chaos."*

"You trust your agents?" Alexander asked.

"They trust me more than life. And those that don't, I keep close—sometimes the fastest snakes are best caged."

Plans flowed quickly now:

> Ambhi's agents would supply the proper permits and seals to allow disguised Greeks into the city as itinerant traders.
>
> Communications would be minimal; all details relayed just before the act, keeping operatives desperate, focused, and dangerous. "Forewarned agents are weak—cornered ones strike hardest," Ambhi observed coolly, a sentiment not lost on his Macedonian counterpart.

They agreed—if the city defenses wavered, and chaos reigned, Alexander would seize the opportunity to cross the river with his main force, while Purushottama's capital burned in confusion. As insurance, Ambhi would keep loyal men in the palace, ready to open the lesser gate at the agreed hour.

As the meeting ended, Alexander lingered. "You never told me, Ambhi—do you intend to be king, or only the last servant left alive?"
Ambhi's smile was as thin as the blade of a viper. "In storms, only the clever survive. Let us both outlive this flood. The rest is just the business of poets."
They parted with nods—predators in mutual camouflage.
Soon, under the fog of dawn, clusters of foreign 'traders'—some Macedonian, some from distant Bactrian towns loyal to Alexander—moved into Paurava. They carried letters sealed by Ambhi's merchants, paid bribes at minor gates, found humble lodging in roadside taverns and busy sarais. By day they practiced patience, by night they mapped, watched, and waited for word.
Ambhi's embedded men, some in the king's court and others among grain depot guards, made quiet contact—passing coded messages through folded accounts and routine prayers. In the evenings, they met in secret, melting into the restless urban flow, their foreign accents masked by coin and caution. They were a web whose center awaited only the right signal.
Porus and Raja Guru, already wary, took counter-measures. Elite soldiers spread through the city, eyes everywhere, ears straining for any slip or cipher out of place. Markets were watched, temples discreetly guarded, and suspicious gatherings reported at once.
Three 'traders' were caught—one at the city well, another buying poison, the third at a whispering gate. One choked on poison before he could be searched. The second, under grueling interrogation, gasped out only, *"There will be attacks... among the innocent.* " Before he could say more, a traitor among Porus's own guard snapped his neck, feigning an accident in the struggle.
The sole escapee, wounded in the flight, limped west and huddled by the river—soon ferried back to Alexander's camp by Ambhi's own trusted men. There, he relayed the

heightened vigilance in Paurava and news of their fellows' capture.

Ambhi, ever careful, saw a problem in loose threads. The escapee did not last the night—found strangled in his tent, Ambhi's message clear: none would compromise the plan, willingly or not.

In the days that followed, both camps moved with the tautness of a drawn arrow. Alexander's men grew tense but restless; Ambhi's operatives in the capital lived with daggers beneath their cloaks and stones on their hearts.

Within Paurava, Purushottama rarely slept. Reports from Veerabhalla and the elite undercover unit arrived hourly. Plans were made to guard key civilian leaders, secure the market grain stores, and prepare for mass confusion, whatever shape it took.

Raja Guru muttered ancient prayers beneath his breath, watching the darkening moon night after night. *"Amāvasyā, Maharaj—a time when even the gods avert their gaze. The silence may be more deadly than the cry."*

Porus could feel the attack coming as surely as rain-laden air signals the coming storm. But how, where, and when—that, even he did not know.

And so, two worlds waited:

One with the patience of traitors.

The other with the steel of the desperate.

High above, mist drifted across the swollen Hydaspes. On both banks, men wondered which gods would answer when the night turned black and men's hearts raced with violence.

Soon, the river would have its answer.

Chapter 15: The Brink of Shadow

Night had draped its velvet shroud over Alexander's riverside command, the only movement the shifting embers and fitful flares of torches. Within the privacy of a taut-draped war tent, two kings sat opposite—one crowned with restless ambition, the other with cold calculation.

The lamp-glow distorted Ambhi's features into something subtle and predatory as he unfurled the city's plans. In the hush, Alexander listened, his blue eyes wary but intrigued—no longer seeing just a nervous ally, but a mind practiced in cunning.

Ambhi's voice was low and certain. *"We strike just before midnight. When street dogs howl and all but the most frightened are lost to dreams. I've marked where our men will sleep, eat, wait. Some—disguised as grain porters, pawnbrokers, ferrymen—will slip through the merchant alleys. Others have already bribed their way past the guards at the southern gate."*

He traced lines on the map with a slender reed. *"We set fires in the quarter where the rich hoard barley, gold, and silk. The flames will draw soldiers and crowds. Simultaneous, my best men and your chosen fifty—hard-eyed, quick—descend on Paurava's grain masters and the leaders of trade guilds. Their deaths will rattle every coin in the city. Make it look like banditry; let rumor do the rest."*

Alexander's attention sharpened at the next stroke. *"And for the heart?"*

Ambhi's gaze flicked upward. *"Ten men—mine and yours—will breach the palace. If they take Porus, the city falls with him. If not, chaos will at least buy time: everyone will be fighting a different fire."*

He paused. *"After two hours, they must vanish—no trophies, no stray tongues. If captured, they die with my seal on their lips. No word of our names, or Paurava will rally the other kingdoms to war. We must be ghosts—leaving only fear behind."*

It was ruthless and clever, and Alexander recognized a peer's mind at work. He nodded once, the flicker in his eye conceding respect even as he weighed betrayal.

"You bargain with men as if they are stones on a go board, Ambhi."
Ambhi gave a humorless smile. *"One wins board games with sacrifices, not sympathy."*
A final grip of hands sealed the pact—two predators, each watching for the other's teeth.
Across the river, beneath Paurava's flickering lamps, all was wary readiness. In the palace war room, Porus, Veerabhalla, Raja Guru, and the grizzled court elders surveyed reports and counter-plans with sleepless eyes.
"Post a runner at every blue-tiled well and every temple gate—if fire or blood, they ring the bells and summon help," Porus commanded. *"If the palace is targeted, let them think me vulnerable. My life means less than a thousand innocents."*
"But Maharaj..." Veerabhalla insisted, frustrated, *"if you die, the city falls! Keep your Black Guard close—"*
Porus shook his head. *"They'll protect the markets. If chaos erupts, the people must see some order stand. Let the king risk his blood; the kingdom must keep its hope."*
Raja Guru intoned ancient verses, anointing door-lintels with turmeric and sandal, placing iron amulets by the thresholds. *"Victory does not belong to those who fear shadows. It belongs to those who shine their lamp upon them."*
In the alleys and lanes, palace soldiers—some in plain dhotis or ragged tunics—watched, waited, and marked faces. Veerabhalla himself roamed the grain markets and river ghats, shrouded, his sword hidden in a sack of onions.
The city knew something was coming. The tension was not named but felt: bakers tightened iron bolts, mothers kept children from windows, the gates all double-locked, and even thieves took the night off.
In the outer sprawl of the city, Alexander's disguised men filtered in: a burly Thracian passing as a wrestler, a Ptolemaic archer haggling in broken Punjabi, a silent

Bactrian courier pretending to sell dates. Seals from Ambhi's traders bought them cover, and gold bought silence.
As Ambhi's final message spread—hidden in baskets, folded in accounts, lips to ears in the city's wine shops—the code was clear:
"Sleep in shadow. Wait for the city's lamps to die before you move. Do as the plan commands. Survive—but if you are caught, speak only dust."
By midnight, the wind carried a strange, expectant scent—spiced with oil, sweat, anxiety, and, somewhere unspoken, the threat of burning.
Porus, on the palace balcony, looked out across his city. Lamps dotted the darkness, more vulnerable than ever before. Somewhere out there, he knew, invisible hands poised over blades waited for the bell to toll.
"Tonight," he whispered, pressing his palm to the cool marble, *"the gods will measure courage. Tomorrow, the land remembers only those who stood their ground."*
In the temple, Raja Guru kept vigil, low chanting drifting to the already sleepless stars.

Chapter 16: The Night of Knives

The new moon draped Paurava in absolute darkness. Even the stars seemed swallowed by a thick veil of clouds. The city, once vibrant with the rhythms of trade and prayer, now shivered beneath a heavy silence—one thick with dread and anticipation.
Amid the shadows, Ambhi and Alexander's men—disguised as humble traders, artisans, and pilgrims—rooted themselves in the city's arteries, waiting for the signal. Their weapons lay hidden beneath cloaks and in baskets, their eyes fiery with the promise of violence.
A wagon laden with barley exploded near the eastern merchant quarter. Flames roared skyward, licking at wooden carts and spreading like a malevolent beast.

Two oxen, panicked, tore free from their harnesses, charging blindly through narrow lanes. Their frantic escape overturned spice stalls, scattering blackened peppercorns and shattering clay jars. Civilians screamed in terror as fire leapt from roof to roof.

Masked raiders surged from alleys, blades flashing. A young boy running with a frightened dog was slashed in the ankle, collapsing on the cobblestones. An elderly shopkeeper grasped a broom like a spear but was struck down before he could defend his wife.

Purushothama 's soldiers snapped into motion, sprinting toward the chaos. The narrow streets echoed with the clash of steel and shouts of defiance. A grandmother, silver hair wild, hurled a clay water pot against a raider's forehead, cracking his skull and buying moments for a cornered child to flee. Nearby, market boys seized benches and poles, driving back attackers with desperate courage. Blood stained the ground, but cries rose:

"To me! Hold them back!"

In Goldsmiths' Lane, a family fractured by fear and rage barricaded their clay-walled home. The merchant, a man once proud of fine silks and shimmering gems, tried to protect his wife and daughters.

Raiders smashed through the door, demanding coin and valuables.

"Take what you want—but spare the children!" the merchant begged.

One brute raised a burning torch to the thatch roof, and the family's world drowned in smoke and screams. The merchant's blood stained the dust; his daughters were dragged screaming into dark alleys.

Neighbors rushed to intervene. An undercover soldier burst in, sword flashing like lightning, cutting down one attacker and forcing a retreat. The desperate defender drove his knees into a cornered looter's ribs while nearby, the community's anger kindled into fierce resistance.

Near the southeastern granary, a wealthy grain trader's home became a bloodied tableau of terror. His son was stabbed before he could stand, a wife thrown aside while begging for mercy.

Raiders demanded keys to the grain storage, sending sacks of precious rice and lentils into flames. Servants who fled were cut down. When neighbors finally arrived, the courtyard was ablaze; only sorrow and ruin remained.

In a narrow tunnel near the temple district, an old beggar woman crouched beside her injured son. Clutching a battered bowl, their only treasure, they were helpless before three masked men.

"Please, take nothing. Spare us," she pleaded.

The attackers laughed cruelly, overturning the bowl and stabbing the boy. The mother screamed but was shoved aside, falling silent as the men disappeared into the night.

At the heart of the grain market, traders held a tense meeting—discussion of rationing and reserves turned to horror as raiders burst in. The men pleaded, but steel answered.

A dozen lay dead on the blood-spattered floor; sacks of grain burned, ledgers consumed. The attackers' goal was destruction of both wealth and will, striking the city's economic core.

On the fringes of the wealthy quarter, a kind but cautious moneylender was cornered and slaughtered. His widow crawled to his side, crying out. The invaders took his gold but left sorrow and fear as lasting spoils.

All over Paurava, terror clashed with defiance.

Some hid behind bolted doors, whispering prayers. Others, fueled by desperation and loyalty, seized farm tools, stones, and kitchen knives to join the fight.

Children tossed rocks; women poured boiling water; old men swung incense staffs, their chanting rising with each battle cry.

"Purushothama fights for us!" came the word. *"The king fights with us!"*
Voices grew louder, hearts steadier. Defenders rallied where before they would have fled.
Within the marble halls, where gold gleamed cold and statues watched silent witness, Porus met his challengers.
Ten assassins moved like ghosts through grand corridors. Some bore Indian garb, others Greek armor. Their leader hissed:
"For Ambhi and Alexander—tonight, Paurava falls."
Porus, unshaken, gripped his sword. *"Show me who sent you, or fall by my hand."*
Battle erupted—blades flashing in the flickering torchlight, bodies striking marble and floor.
Porus danced through attacks, every move honed from years of battle and training in kalarippayattu. He twisted an arm, snapped it with a crack, disarmed foes, and sent one crashing into a burning brazier. Blows whistled past him; he countered with swift kicks, precise strikes, and deadly counters.
An attacker raved, *"This is punishment! We reign tonight!"*
Porus sneered. *"You die for betrayal."*
After twenty minutes of ferocious combat, eight men lay dead; one broken survived, bound for questioning.
Porus strode from the hall, bloodied but victorious, and prepared to meet the wider battle beyond.
Raja Guru, once a warrior himself, donned mail and charged into the chaos alongside Veerabhalla.
"Archers, to the towers! Raise the walls!" he commanded.
From rooftops, arrows lit the night sky, cutting down invaders. Guards raised barricades; townsfolk formed fighting bands. Mothers protected children; youths brandished whatever weapons they could find.
In one narrow street, Veerabhalla's men confronted attackers attempting to burn the water tower. Steel clashed, and by dawn only the wounded remained.

Everywhere, the city fought—not just soldiers, but its entire soul.
As dawn painted the sky crimson, the smoke of burning homes and granaries curled skyward.
28 civilians lay dead.
130 injured cried for aid.
12 soldiers had fallen.
Over half the attackers lay slain or captured; some had fled into shadows.
Porus walked amidst the wounded and grieving, offering prayers and words of comfort.
"Your courage saved this city," he said softly. *"I mourn those lost, but promise no more shall fall for lack of will."*
The people cried out in renewed hope:
"Jai Paurava! Jai Maharaj Purushothama!"
Raja Guru knelt in scattered ashes, chanting rites, binding the living to memory and resolve.
Veerabhalla's hands shook with sweat and blood, yet his eyes burned with fury and pride.
Porus turned to his commanders:
"We survived the wolf's night—now must we hunt the jackals who hide in our midst."

Chapter 17: Dawn of Resolve

The sunrise after the night of knives brought more grief than hope. The city woke to streets still shimmering with ash and blood, the clang of hammers fixing splintered doors blending with the keening of widows. Everywhere, mothers, sisters, and wives wept for sons and husbands—some lost to death, others to captivity or wandering, some to the raw hunger of ruined granaries. Yet amidst mourning, a fierce resolve rose: this was not simply revenge, but the unwavering need to defend home, to protect what blood and soil had made sacred.

King Purushothama's soldiers and court officers marched through the battered capital—not as conquerors, but as kin. They offered prayers at doorways, consoled the grieving, delivered loaves of bread and sacks of grain to those who had lost everything. Artisans aided the repair of homes and markets, while the king ordered community kitchens and temporary shelters be raised—no family was to go hungry or unsheltered while the city healed.

By mid-morning, the great gates of Paurava were shut on all outsiders. Guards turned back traders and travelers with gentle firmness—by the king's command, nothing would disturb the city's fragile regathering.

That day's court opened under a black cloud. Porus entered the hall, meeting the eyes of those who remained. Gaps along the benches marked the men and women who would never return. The air throbbed with anger, pain, and purpose.

Veerabhalla, bloodied but unbowed, stood first:

"Maharaj, the attack began at the merchant quarter, spread to the grain markets and palace itself. Our soldiers rallied quickly. We lost 40 souls—12 soldiers, 28 civilians. More than 130 wounded –49 of them warriors. Their chaos was met with iron: seventy of their bandits fell, and we have captured fourteen—though thirteen still live. We must shake the truth from their tongues."

Next rose the Minister of Treasury—Dhanapati Yajnavalkya, a shrewd-faced elder: *"O King, the treasury itself is safe—but the city bleeds gold and grain. Eight market streets burned. Damage to the fortress and public infrastructure is 4,000 gold panas; losses among the wealthy and merchant families nearly 15,000 panas in stolen coin, spices, gems, destroyed property—some fortunes ruined forever. If these raids go unchecked, famine or poverty could follow the war."*

Porus nodded gravely. "All damages, public and private, shall be compensated from the royal coffers. No tax shall be collected until this storm passes."

A ripple of astonished relief swept the room—but Dhanapati dared respond, voice tinged with anxiety: *"Your mercy is legend, Maharaj. But without taxes, what fuels the arsenal, feeds the camps, pays for grain?"* Porus lifted his chin. *"War will not be the yoke of the people. There are other reserves; we will find trade or aid, but not a single coin shall be squeezed from these wounds."* Some clapped in admiration, others in lingering doubt. The court then discussed security, food supplies, rumors of unrest, and the need for more patrols.

When the court emptied, only Porus, Raja Guru Devadatta, and Veerabhalla lingered. Porus thanked them both for courage and lamented their shared limits. "We did all we could. But we will do more."

Turning to the matter of the captured enemy, Veerabhalla reported:

"The interrogations began, Maharaj. At first, nothing but venom and silence. But one name surfaced: the officer who questioned the spy last night—he fled in the chaos, and several men saw him. He is an agent of Ambhi. The plot runs deep."

Together, they walked to the interrogation chamber, where fear and pain had cracked the foreign agents' pride. At last, one confessed:

> The sabotage was planned by Ambhi of Taxila and Alexander of Macedon.
>
> He revealed the meet-point where the foreign agents would regroup after the attack—deep in the forest, near an old stone shrine.
>
> He also confirmed the identity and betrayal of the officer who had killed the spy—an embedded traitor in Porus's own ranks.

Porus's eyes hardened. "Then let most of them die. Leave two alive—to show us the path, and to bear a message."

Veerabhalla executed the condemned, left two cowering survivors, and prepared for vengeance.

The following night, Veerabhalla led a handpicked squad into the forest, the two surviving traitors bound and gagged at the front. The moon, two days grown since Amavasya, still struggled to break the darkness. When they reached the enemy hideout—a crude, hidden camp—Veerabhalla tied the guides to a tree to prevent their escape.
With cold discipline, the Paurava warriors unleashed retribution. Fire swept the camp; fleeing enemy agents were cut down, burned, mutilated in a wave of pitiless violence.
As dawn tinged the east, Veerabhalla left two severed heads—one Greek, one Taxilan—in the hands of the surviving traitors.
"Take them," he snarled, "to Alexander and Ambhi. Tell your kings—the son of Bharat will not sleep while jackals hunt in the dark."
When Ambhi received the head of his own man, his heart stammered with dread—he had always known Porus fierce, but never so swift and implacable. For the first time, he doubted his path, and considered moving his court to Alexander's camp before his own allies turned on him.
Alexander, meanwhile, accepted the gory token with a warrior's smirk. Prideful, almost eager, he gave the order to muster arms. *"At last, he answers as a true king," he declared to his council. "Now let the world see whose gods are stronger."*
Trumpets sounded in the Macedonian camp; soldiers sharpened blades and whispered rumors. The stage was set for a reckoning not of traitors or saboteurs—but of kings.

Chapter 18: Gathering the Storm

The city of Paurava breathed heavily under the burden of war's approach. Streets once alive with the careless laughter of children and market cries throbbed now with the clang of hammer on anvil, the low bellow of elephants in training, and the sharp bark of generals drilling cavalry. The scent of freshly oiled leather mingled with incense, prayers, and the smoke of food fires feeding a restless army.

Civilians moved with cautious purpose, packing storerooms with grain, patching broken roofs, and reinforcing city gates. Mothers whispered lessons of courage to wide-eyed children, while elders blessed warriors with murmured chants and amulets. The king's commands rippled through the capital like a drumbeat—every grain weighed, every sword polished, every shadow watched.

King Purushothama himself walked among his people—no longer a distant monarch but a guardian of hearth and home. His hands arranged the distribution of food and shelter, comforted widows, and reassured the worried. By royal decree, the city gates were locked tight against all but essential entry—no traders, no strangers, only those bearing the king's seal might enter.

In the marble-walled court, beneath banners gray with smoke from the last battle, the great war council assembled. Veerabhalla rose with the certainty of a man who wears history in his scars.

"Majesty," he said, eyes sharp as a falcon's, *"our soldiers stand ready—archers, cavalry, war elephants, all trained and waiting your command. The granaries are stocked; the armory groans with weapons. The camps can be established wherever you deem best."*

Porus nodded thoughtfully. The memory of the Night of Knives—fires rising against his city, his people bleeding—pressed upon him. He had once hoped for peace, sought parley and silence in the storms of ambition, but those hopes lay smoldering with burning granaries. The time for hesitation had ended.

" *War* ," he spoke quietly but firmly, " *was never sought by us. But now, the enemy has made it inevitable. We shall protect our subjects with every breath.*"

Messages flew swiftly as hawks sent to the courts of allies: Kalinga, Malava, Magadha, and the tribal chieftains. Reinforcements were promised—grain, archers, warriors—but it was not just steel and numbers that were marshaled. It was the resolve of a land that would not yield.

Far to the west, beyond the swollen currents of the Hydaspes, Alexander's camp rose like a sprawling, restless beast beside the riverbank. Under Ambhi's counsel, it shifted closer to the water's edge, its tents fluttering like the banners of an invading tempest.

Ambhi, with the cold, calculating eyes of a viper, briefed Alexander beneath a tent woven of Persian silks and Macedonian wool.

"To cross the Hydaspes unchallenged ," Ambhi said, voice low and measured, *"we must strike at their expectations. The Paurava believe the river is their guard. If we remain on this side, they wait, watch, and strike in weakness, when hunger and rain sap our strength."*

Alexander nodded, his gaze burning with hunger for conquest.

"We will find a way to cross—and when we do, it will be thunder, not a whisper. Let their watches falter. Let shadow mask our approach."

His engineers had gathered timber for pontoon bridges; scouts practiced silent crossings upstream. Boats were hidden beneath reeds; archers trained to strike swiftly from riverbanks. The Macedonian host adjusted to the unfamiliar heat and insect hum—a foreign life beneath alien skies.

Back in Paurava, the drumbeat of preparations quickened. Officers debated camp placements, weighing supply routes, water sources, and terrain vantage points. Veerabhalla advised on defensive perimeters:

"We must control the high ground near the river. Camouflaged sentries will guard all approaches. Tribal scouts will harry any enemy movement before the main force."

Purushothama listened intently, his thoughts a whirl of strategy and the faces of those he vowed to protect. *"I was hesitant,"* he confessed to Raja Guru one evening as the hall quieted. *"To take up war, to spill blood when peace could still be woven. But the strike on our home left no choice—for now, we fight not for glory, but for survival."* The spiritual sage nodded in solemn accord.

"Let every prayer you utter, Maharaj, be for the strength to keep this land whole. And for the wisdom to wield steel only as last resort."

As the sun set behind copper skies, lightning hinted at the monsoon's promise—nature itself seeming to hold its breath. In camps lit by torch and restless shadows, the tension was shared by all—warriors from distant lands and local tribes, merchants turned warriors, kings turned commanders.

In Paurava's war room, Purushothama stood over the carved map of the Hydaspes. His hand rested on the waters traced in blue, eyes fierce.

"Let the river see this day," he whispered, *"that we stood not as prey beneath hawk and lion, but as the shield of Bharat."* Across the river,

Alexander traced the same waters, eyes aflame. *"Tonight we prepare,"* he breathed. *" Before dawn, the gods themselves may not know which king the river will allow to cross."*

The clash of fates drew near.

Chapter 19: River of Waiting, River of Fate

The land heaved with distant thunder, but it was not rain that made the Macedonians uneasy—it was the jungle itself. Alexander's march through the forest was nothing like the plains of Persia or the valleys of Syria. This was a world of dripping vines and roots that fought every step. Overhead, the constant call of unseen creatures mixed with the endless bite of mosquitoes. The air was thick as wet wool, and every boot found mud or tangled roots. Insects swarmed over the column, biting until soldiers bled raw. For three days, then four, the host pressed east, cutting paths with axes, dragging carts through marsh, their armor dulled by heat and rot. Coughs soon joined the whispers—fevers wracking strong men, sweat soaking padded tunics, eyes reddening. Ambhi sent powders and rare roots, his herb-doctors moving among the sick. Even so, the jungle took its toll: dozens fell to fever, a few to madness, others to wounds that festered too quickly to treat.

Alexander stalked the paths each night, his patience threadbare.

"We must crush Porus before this country kills us for him," he muttered to Hephaestion, as another soldier's body was burned on a pyre beside the trail.

When at last the trees thinned and the forest spat them out, the soldiers beheld the shining breadth of the Hydaspes at dawn—broad, bronze-green, and restless. The river's song was deep and strong, a moving wall between Alexander and his prize. The shore was wide, flat, and gave space for the exhausted army to raise its tents. Camps sprang up in disciplined rows, boats secured and horses watered. But unease haunted every man—here was the edge of the known world, and the river felt as much curse as boundary.

While the Greeks rebuilt their strength on the riverbank, the news flashed across the water: Porus's spies, silent as owls, relayed word of the enemy's arrival, their numbers, their sickness. Within stone-walled chambers, King Purushothama gathered his council—Veerabhalla flashing reports, Raja Guru sharp-eyed, and senior commanders tense at the news.

Porus's voice was steady, but storm-shadowed with thought. The question lingered: Should they attack now, or wait?

Veerabhalla, his face marked by sleepless nights, spoke first.

"Maharaj, the Hydaspes is friend and shield. In this early rainy season, the river's strength is ours. Alexander cannot force a crossing now—not with his men sick and their spirits battered. If we attack, we give up our home ground, throw ourselves at their blades. But if we wait, the monsoon will shatter them first."

Raja Guru added in a tone deep as temple bells:

"Let the river do half our work. In the tales of old, kings who rushed to cross the waters too soon fed the river their pride—and their bones. Let Alexander stew in fever and fear. When the clouds have emptied and his spirit is weakest, then we strike, and not before."

"It is said, the Ganga herself once rose to drown an arrogant king," Raja Guru mused. "This land is patient. Its rivers favor the one who knows when to wait, and when to charge."

Porus agreed, his doubts slowly stilled by the wisdom of old scars:

"Then we wait. Let the enemy learn what Bharat's waters and storms can teach. We'll keep our soldiers sharp, supply lines strong, let the Greeks waste under storm and fever."

Messengers hurried to allied camps: hold supplies, stand alert; the time for battle will come—but only when Porus gives the sign.

As days passed, the mood in Paurava's ranks shifted. The scale of what approached—the greatest war of their age—sent waves of confusion and anxiety through even the bravest warriors. Seasoned men remembered border skirmishes, fierce but quick; this, though, was to be a storm for the ages.

Younger fighters whispered rumors:

"Can even elephants trample foreign steel? Do the gods favor us, or do they sleep?"

Some doubted; others grew tense, silent; only a few boasted, but even their voices rang thin.

Porus and Raja Guru watched this closely. The king kept his silence, letting men find their courage, knowing the best strength is that which survives doubt. For nearly a week, the men drilled, built palisades, and checked arrow stores. The city's smiths burned through their nights forging spear tips and chariot axles. The wheat and rice was counted, the mounts watered, the war elephants washed and oiled until they gleamed like living monoliths.

When the time was right, Porus called all commanders, chieftains, officers, and warriors to the high courtyard beneath the palace. Lamps swayed in the evening breeze. The sky was blue-black with the first blush of monsoon clouds.

Raja Guru stood forward, staff in hand, his voice both gentle and thunderous:

"You fear, because you are wise. You wait, because you are strong. This river has not seen such an army in a thousand seasons... but it is not the first battle she has watched, nor will it be the last.

Let me tell you, before this great night, of a king from our very own land—a time when foes from every direction crossed our rivers, and all seemed lost.

...Hear now the tale of the War of Ten Kings—how Bharat once stood against a flood of fire, and what strength truly means..."
As the men pressed closer, hungry for courage and legend, the story began—binding the present moment to ancient memory, weaving hope from the scars of history.

Chapter 20: Dāśarājña Yajña — The Sacrifice and the Storm

A deep silence wrapped the Paurava camp. The torches snapped, the drums faded, and every soldier's heart drummed in his chest. Commanders, chieftains, and even the king himself leaned in toward Raja Guru Devadatta, who stood floodlit by the sacred fire, eyes glinting with the wisdom of a thousand harvests.
His staff struck stone, and his voice was thunder and prophecy intertwined:
"O warriors of Bharat! You gather on this sacred riverbank, wondering if your strength will endure, if courage can outlast destiny. Let me tell you: this is not the first dawn when every clan shook in fear, nor the first time the rivers bore witness to blood and sacrifice. Before Alexander's name was whispered, before even the word 'Paurava' rang from gate to gate, the rivers themselves chose the bravest from among men. Listen to the legend of the Dāśarājña Yajña—the War of Ten Kings, when all Bharat trembled on the edge of a blade!"
"In the mist-wrapped cradle of a younger world, the land we call our own was a tapestry of proud rajas—each coveting his border, each crowned by ancestry and ambition. The clans: Druhyu, Anu, Puru, Matsya, Bhalanas, Alinas, and others, each ruled from high-walled fortresses, each eyeing their neighbors with envy and dread.

But among them was Sudās, king of the Bharatas—a man raised not just for war, but for dharma. His court echoed with the songs of rishis, and his rule brought peace—or so it seemed.

Where the river Paruṣṇī (the modern Ravi) curved like a blade across the plains, Sudās ruled his people: he irrigated fields, built shrines, hosted yajñas that drew sages from as far as distant Gandhara. But his rise alarmed the other rulers, for Sudās's fame was growing too fast, his fields too green, his allies too loyal.

Rumors turned to fear, fear to talk, and talk to alliance. Nine kings—stubborn, fierce, brilliant and haughty—bound their destinies together, swearing before the sacrificial fires to crush Sudās at any cost.

A dawn came when ten banners darkened the horizon."

"Rivers flowed thick with haste; drums sounded in ten fortresses; kshatriyas painted their faces with ghee and blood, vowing their line would not end. They swore this was not war, but yajña—a sacrifice not of mere goats, but of hatred, vengeance, and pride itself, poured into the fire until one king was left standing.

The ten kings convened their priests—not merely for omens, but to summon the full force of prayer and curse. Their yajña fires rose, thick with offerings, as mantras twisted through the winds, blending with schemes and whispered bribes.

Each king brought something to the pact—chariots like flowing rivers, archers as numerous as cranes, elephants draped in silver bells, and warriors drunk on destiny.

The alliance was stitched with suspicion—each king dreaming of victory, each secretly fearing the others' betrayal should Sudās falter."

"King Sudās saw the shadow on his border; his own court split, with some urging retreat, others demanding blind attack. But his greatest ally was his rishi-counselor, Vashistha—the voice of memory and hope.

Vashistha said: 'Do not meet fire with fire, but with purpose. War is a yajña. Sacrifice not only in flame, but in courage and rightness. Offer not grain or gold, but the will to endure, even when all seems lost.'

Sudās listened, and summoned his faithful: the Mahabharata poets, the horsemen of the plains, the women who crafted shields by moonlight, and the children who fetched arrows from the city's edge. Before the sacred fire, he swore: 'I do not fight for conquest, but for the honor of my land and the peace of my people. If I am to fall, let it be facing the world, knees unbent.'"

"The ten kings marshaled on the west bank—their armies a wall of spears, the earth itself trembling beneath their footsteps. The alliance stretched as far as the eye could see: Puru and the mighty Druhyus blazing as vanguard, Alinas and Bhalanas guarding the flanks, others fanning out like thunderclouds ready to unleash their wrath.

A tempest brewed. Sudās's force held the river crossing, watching as the enemies' chariots lined up in their thousands. At dawn, a thick fog masked the river—horses stamped, chariots creaked, men prayed, and priests on both sides hurled mantras and curses.

Suddenly, the signal: horns blared, war drums burst. Arrows screamed from every direction. Spears clashed. Chariots thundered into the torrent, wheels splitting mud, warriors bellowing their ancestral names.

But the river itself became a force. As Sudās's allies invoked Indra, the storm-god, dark clouds swept in. Lightning struck—some say as a sign, others as mere chance, but on that day, fate became a weapon.

Rain roared, turning the ground beneath the boots of the ten kings into a morass. The enemy's chariots bogged and twisted, their elephants slipping on the churned river-mud. Arrows faltered. Trumpeters lost bearings. The alliance wavered as erstwhile friends now jostled for position, desperate to avoid their own men's horses in the chaos."

"In that drowned chaos, Sudās's warriors pressed forward—chariots slicing left, blades flashing. Drums of dharma thundered alongside the pulses of battle. The alliance of ten, built on greed and suspicion, fractured as kings accused each other of cowardice, betrayal, and hoarding glory.

One by one, leaders fell: Puru struck down by a Bharata archer, Druhyu's elephant crushed beneath a collapsed war cart, the Matsya's bow snapped in a whirlpool of blood.

Sudās advanced not with arrogance, but with relentless unity—his men fighting as one, none retreating, each trusting the other not for command, but by the strength of shared sacrifice.

When at last the rains slowed and the river ran red with memory, the alliance was broken. Kings drowned; banners lost. Sudās, battered yet unbowed, stood victorious—not just over men, but destiny. The Paruṣṇī bore away shields, swords, and the bones of prideful kings. From the storm, a new Bharat was forged—a land not united by fear, but by the promise that, when the world unites against us, our courage will prove indivisible."

Raja Guru's voice fell to a whisper that brushed every ear, every waiting heart: *"That victory—born of purpose, sacrifice, unity—lives in your blood. As Sudās once faced the ten kings, so do you now face the tempest beyond this river. Remember: it was not numbers, nor gold, nor even the loudest prayer that won the day—it was the yajña of hearts, the burning of fear into pride, the unbreakable bond of kinship in the face of oblivion.*

Today, YOU are Sudās's heirs. Today, the Hydaspes waits to carve your names beside those of the ancients."

A great waft of awe and silence swept the crowd.

Veerabhalla's fist hardened over his sword. Young archers rose taller. Across the torchlit banks, men and women gripped hands and whispered to one another:

"We are the children of those who conquered ten kings."

Raja Guru closed, staff lifted to the sky:

"Let this yajña begin—not of blood alone, but of will and unity! The rivers watch. The ancestors watch. Fight not for vengeance, but for destiny!"

The silence cracked, a roar rose, and the army of Paurava felt, for a moment, unconquerable—knowing they carried more than weapons into battle—they carried the living legend of Bharat.

Chapter 21: The River That Waits

The story of the *Daśarājña Yajña* had spread like sacred fire through the camp. Around evening hearths, in barrack lines, beside the elephant pens, soldiers retold the tale to one another — of King Sudās defying ten allied kings, of rivers turned to allies, of unity forged in flood and fire.

Men who had earlier doubted now spoke with hard eyes. Youths checked their bowstrings twice as often. Veterans inspected their armor as if repairing a family heirloom. By dawn, the Paurava host was not just prepared; it was eager. The Hydaspes would remember their name.

In the palace war hall, incense coiled around the vaulted roof as King Purushottama sat flanked by Raja Guru Devadatta and General Veerabhalla, with senior commanders and ministers forming a half-circle before them.

On the sand-map table, wooden markers shaped like horses, elephants, and spears showed the positions of friendly forces along the capital's roads, walls, and northern routes.

Veerabhalla broke the silence first.

"Maharaj, the obvious choice is to take the entire army to the riverside and meet Alexander head-on. But if we strip the city

bare, we invite a dagger to our own chest. Should the enemy feign an advance, cross elsewhere, or slip inside through Ambhi's treachery, Paurava will fall without a fight."

Porus nodded gravely.

"If the city falls, we lose the war — no matter the river's victory."
Raja Guru traced the river-line on the map with his staff.
"We station our main body along the riverbank so the enemy never doubts we watch them. Yet leave a strong garrison in the city — enough to fight off any infiltration or sudden crossing attempts. Ambhi and Alexander both have the mind for feints. We will deny them that advantage."

The plan was set — the Hydaspes bank would bear the shield of Paurava, but the citadel's heart would remain guarded. Since the infiltration during the Night of Knives, security in the capital had grown unyielding. Veerabhalla's hidden watchers swept the markets, wells, and caravanserais. In three days, they seized every operative Ambhi had managed to slip in. Some were executed immediately — their loyalty beyond redemption — while a handful were thrown into deep cells, kept breathing long enough to spill every detail of Ambhi's plans.
Word of this spread quietly, bolstering morale: the snake's fangs in the city had been blunted.
From every road into the capital, allies now came — tall Kalinga lancers in lacquered armor, Malava mahouts with their own towering elephants, tribal archers daubed in green and brown, blending living forest into the army's lines.
By the king's count, the host stood at:

30,000 infantry — spearmen, swordsmen, and archers.
4,000 cavalry — light horse for flanking, heavy cavalry for shock.
200 war elephants — each armored in iron and bronze, tusks capped and painted with protective mantras.

Each unit was placed beneath commanders who knew both the men and the land they would bleed on.
The war-feel had settled over the capital like storm-clouds.
At temples, civilians offered flowers, ghee lamps, and prayers to Devi and Deva, whispering the names of husbands, brothers, and sons due to march.
The cry was the same everywhere: *"Let the gods guard them and bring them home."*
The next morning, the king ordered the entire army — commanders, standard-bearers, cavalry captains, elephant-drivers — to gather within the great courtyard.
Priests in saffron robes stood before sacrificial mounds. The air smelled of incense, blood, and wet earth as bisons were offered to Bhairava, Durga, and Indra — gods of storm, war, and protection.
Chants rose like rolling thunder:
"May your right hand know no hesitation!
May your eyes see only the path to victory!"
When the consecrations ended, Raja Guru summoned Veerabhalla.
The old master spoke in low, steady tones — the full plan: which divisions would guard the city, which would take the riverbank, where the elephants would form the deterrent wall, and where flexibility must be kept for surprise maneuvers.
Veerabhalla, as protocol demanded, relayed every instruction to the assembled field-commanders.
At the blast of the conch, the army began to move. The sound was awe-inspiring — iron-tipped spears clashing in cadence,

cavalry hooves like rolling drums, war-oxen groaning under supply carts, the deep chest-rumble of elephants.
Every tree branch quivered, every bird took flight.
Children and elders lined the streets, throwing flowers, touching the dust raised by the king's mount to their foreheads. For two full days, the column wound its way down the river road — a living serpent of bronze, leather, and steel.
On the third day, the Paurava host reached the wide, grassy eastern bank of the Hydaspes. Camps sprang up in disciplined rows:

> Elephant lines reinforced with stout bamboo palisades.
> Archer watchtowers erected within hours.
> Supply tents placed out of arrow range.
> Signal fires prepared for instant communication with the city garrison.

Across the glimmering waters, Alexander's camp lay in full view — its tents like pale teeth in the landscape, banners snapping in the damp breeze. The two armies now watched each other with unblinking attention.
The monsoon had begun. Warm rain drummed on tent roofs and swelled the river until its currents snarled and churned. Crossing now was dangerous — to boat or to man — and both sides knew it.
Porus saw at once the advantage: the longer they waited, the greater the toll of fever, insects, and wet-weather rot on Alexander's men. Already, spies whispered that Greek soldiers were falling to flux and coughing sickness. Alexander, too, would see the same truth. That meant the days ahead would be a contest of patience, deception, and will.
And so, the Hydaspes became a mirror — each bank reflecting the other's readiness, testing its nerve without a single arrow loosed.

It was not yet the day of battle.
But looking at the swollen, churning river between them, every man could feel it — *the river was not the only thing waiting to break.*

Chapter 22: When the River Spoke

The Hydaspes was no longer a river.
It was a breathing wall of fury, swollen by the late monsoon, roaring like a war-drum of the gods themselves. Its currents spun in violent eddies, dragging whole trunks of trees downstream and shattering them against hidden rocks. No man dared cross, not even under orders, not even under hunger. Even Alexander, storm-breaker of empires, horse-lord of the world, stood waiting upon its banks. The river mocked his urgency, as though telling him: *Not yet, conqueror. Not until I decree.*
Across the water, two worlds stared at each other. On the western bank, Alexander's vast camp spread in ordered lines, its soldiers restless under rain, their bronze helms dull in the monsoon haze. Supplies rotted in damp crates; horses, unused to thick Indian humidity, stamped and frothed under disease. Where once discipline had been perfect, now came coughing, blistered skin, and weary voices muttering in too many tongues. Small flare-ups of discontent were crushed with ruthless efficiency: rations withheld, deserters flogged, and a few strung up on makeshift gibbets as reminders that *Alexander tolerated no weakness* .

And yet, beneath the punishment, morale strained. Men who had crossed deserts and seas began to ask: "Why one more king? Why one more battle, when we could march home instead?"

Ambhi of Taxila moved tirelessly among the sick-beds, bringing herbs and physicians from his land, feeding the Greek officers with honeyed words and gilt promises. His face was one of loyalty, but to every Paurava soul, his name had already become *the fox beneath the tent* .
On the eastern bank, King Purushottama's camp stood calmer, steadier. Watchtowers had been built high in the trees along the shore, their lookout fires glowing through the rains. From there, scouts recorded the smallest stir in Alexander's camp—the rolling of wagons, the building of rafts, the sudden silencing of sections of the army.
The Paurava soldiers were calm, sharpened like blades kept sheathed before their day. They had hope, and they had their king who fought beside them in the training fields. They knew their elephants did not fear storms, and their bows found strength in dampened air. If the river calmed, they planned to cross first, pushing into the western forests where the Macedonian phalanx would be weakest. *Let Alexander learn what it meant to fight where soil itself fought back.*

Every night, braziers burned high in the towers on both sides, but no man dared set a boat afloat. Crossing meant certain death—drowned in the fury of the river, or dashed and broken like a child's toy. Even spies kept back; the Hydaspes was uncrossable. And so, the only reports either king could trust came from watchers' eyes glittering through wet leaves, mirrored in silence by their enemy across the torrent.

Each camp became obsessed with observing the other, each army boiling under the tension of waiting.

Alexander's high command gathered nightly under the sagging roof of the war tent. Hephaestion, steadfast, advised patience: "When the waters shrink, we cross, orderly and whole—strike then."

But others—Ptolemy, Seleucus, and the grimmer officers—warned that fever gnawed the ranks. The monsoon was killing more men than Persian spears had ever done. Idleness bred treachery, silence bred despair. *They must move, or risk collapse.*
It was Ambhi who leaned nearest to Alexander, whispering like poison.

"The river will not calm soon. But storms can hide us. Cross not when the river is gentle, but when the skies weep most fierce. Who will expect it? When your ships and horses vanish in thunder, when lightning blinds their watchtowers — then, O Alexander, you will stand on the far shore before Porus can breathe."

The generals murmured — dangerous, risky, but not without genius. Alexander's blue eyes narrowed, gleaming with that cold fire that had outlasted Persia, Greece, and Egypt.

"Yes. Not despite the storm... but with it. We become the storm." Now their problem was focus. How to draw Porus's gaze while the true crossing occurred elsewhere?
Plans spiraled from their lips:

> Setting fires along one flank to deceive his archers.
> Marching cavalry openly near one ford while secretly crossing another.
> Using elephants captured in Persia to create false trumpets.

Alexander's mind stitched the ideas into design. They would *shroud in chaos, and pierce with silence* .
Meanwhile, Porus convened his own councils by torchlight in rain-soaked tents. Raja Guru listed every possible move Alexander might attempt: feints, diversions, false night marches. Veerabhalla thumped the table once.

"Let him try. If he crosses upstream, elephants will break him in the forest. If he crosses downstream, our cavalry will pin him in the marsh. If he dares the center, the river will have him before we need to lift a spear."

Porus, silent, only gazed at the river through the mist.

"No conqueror comes without teeth. He will not wait meekly. He will choose guile. And so—we wait for his shadow to betray him."
Days passed. The river still raged. The camps roared with drill, with prayer, with rain.
Neither king moved.
Neither king blinked.

But all men—Greek, Indian, ally, traitor—knew one truth: The storm would decide. And when its voice fell silent, the Hydaspes would drink blood enough to remember until the end of time.

Chapter 23: When the Storm Became the Battlefield

The monsoon had fully claimed the skies, unleashing relentless storms that tore through the landscape like furious gods. The Hydaspes, swollen and wild, churned with a deadly energy that turned the river into a roaring beast, its waters rising and falling with terrifying unpredictability. To watch it was to stare into the face of death itself—timeless, indifferent, merciless.

On the eastern bank, the Paurava warriors stood unbowed, battle-hardened by seasons of such storms. Rain-soaked leather and mud-clad feet were familiar foes, their spirits tempered like the iron of their spears. The elephants, armored and unflinching, trumpeted defiance into the howling wind. Soldiers tightened grips on bows and swords, their eyes sharp despite the tempest.

Across the river, Alexander's camp crumbled under the weight of foreign skies. The unaccustomed damp clung to flesh and armor, sapping strength and will. Fevers swept through the ranks like a silent scythe, and the groans of the sick rose above clashing thunder. Ambhi of Takshashila moved tirelessly through the chaos, an ever-present shadow of calculated calm, his whispered promises sealing fragile loyalties that trembled as much as the storm-wracked tents. Death had begun its slow tally among the Greeks, though word was barred from crossing the river to Porus. Alexander's iron will demanded that the Indian king believe the enemy stood unbroken, still invincible—fear a weapon no less sharp than any spear.

Yet desperation brewed in the councils of Macedon. The crushing weight of unseen enemies—weather, sickness, and the merciless river—forced Alexander's hand towards decisions long deferred. He summoned Ambhi and his commanders inside the largest tent, their faces etched with resolve and weariness.

"We cannot linger," Alexander declared, his voice barely above the storm's roar. *"The Hydaspes will not yield, and neither can we. Time slips through our fingers, lives with it. We must find a way across, or the army will perish without battle."*

Ambhi, ever cautious yet bold in his cunning, nodded slowly. *"There is a place upriver, some twenty kilometers from here. The river bends and shallows there—its breadth narrows, and its depth is less treacherous. It is risky, and it will take days for scouting, but it may be our path."*

Alexander turned sharply. *"Send men—small, swift squads. Let them move from deep within the forest, parallel to the river's course. They must find this crossing, and any others we might use. Move unseen as shadows. Three days. Then they return, with or without news."*

The generals exchanged solemn glances and agreed. Thus, under the cloak of torrential rain and whispered thunder, detachments vanished into the jungle's oppressive green, swallowed by a wildness the Macedonian soldiers could barely navigate.

Meanwhile, on the eastern shore, Porus, Raja Guru Devadatta, and General Veerabhalla observed the rage of the Hydaspes with gravity. The river's fury was a shield, but also a prison. Intelligence from spies was scarce—jungle and storm blinded their eyes. From afar, the turmoil within Alexander's camp was clear: tents collapsed under heavy downpours, disarray reigned, and soldiers' spirits faltered beneath a siege of nature far harsher than any sword.

The Indian leaders remained vigilant, expecting the fight to come to them head-on. They readied defenses, reinforcing

positions along the riverbank and within the city, unaware of the silent and stealthy probes threading through the jungle across the water.
For days, the river's voice thundered and the storms bled into night. But neither king moved openly. The coming battle, they knew, would not be decided by courage alone—but by who could master the storm itself.

Chapter 24: Crossing the Unyielding Hydaspes

Four groups of scouts, each five strong, mounted their horses at dawn, their eyes heavy with determination despite the rain-soaked jungle they were about to enter. Two rode upriver, two down, threading cautiously through the dense monsoon forest, their path slick with mud and tangled roots. The false ease of the canopy's shadows did little to hide the bitter challenge ahead. Each thunderous step of their horses sank deep, as if the very earth sought to swallow them whole.

Dragged by relentless purpose, they pushed forward through the suffocating green, checking each winding curve of the river's turbulent flow. The Hydaspes surged with relentless fury, swollen by rains that swelled its veins to bursting. Day turned to night and back again, the jungle echoing with unseen creatures and the distant roar of churning waters. After a day's desperate trek, the groups converged at the spot named in Ambhi's secret scroll: a narrow stretch where the river's wrath seemed slightly tamed—a shallow channel bordered by jagged rocks and twisted tree roots. Here, the water whispered danger, swift and merciless, ready to drown any who miscalculated…but it was not impassable. The soldiers studied its depth, the shifting stones beneath the surface, the current's relentless pull.

They weighed every peril.
From this place, bold strategies were born.
A risky crossing lay ahead—one that demanded courage as fierce as the river's resolve. The scouts mapped angles, marked hidden eddies, and noted where fallen giants of wood could be wielded to craft a shallow bridge. The prospect of stepping stones and temporary rafts took shape in their minds—fragile but tangible.
Upriver, the scouts found no sure fords; the river fought every inch fiercely. But far downstream, a different chance emerged—a spot where the river bed shallowed over a wider stretch. Here, great trunks and branches could be lashed into a makeshift bridge. Yet, it was unstable, unfit for the press of horses or the march of a large army. Only a handful of soldiers could brave this crossing before its collapse.
They encoded this fragile hope into mental maps and private words, pressing the knowledge close as they turned back through the treacherous forest, the muddy earth sucking at their boots with every step.
Back at camp, anticipation mingled with restraint. Alexander met their return with a storm of emotion—a flicker of hope shadowed by the fearsome respect the river commanded. His mind, sharpened by conquest, wrestled with this new adversary: nature itself. How could a son of Macedon, master of worlds, face a force untamed and immutable?
Yet the scouts' words rekindled a fire within him.
By the next dawn, the warriors stood before their king, voices grave but triumphant.
"Well, sire," the lead scout reported, *"the river is fierce—death waits in its depths. But in ambush, there is passage. Risky, but real. We found a shallow, narrow crossing where wood and steel could bridge the fury."*
Alexander's cobalt eyes sparked with decision.
"Good," he said, rising to summon his commanders. *"This is the thread we grab. Our fate hangs upon how well we weave from it."*

Gathered beneath the tent's heavy silks, generals and engineers leaned over maps drawn anew with the scouts' findings.

Hephaestion traced the narrow passage with a finger. *"We may build rafts and bridge frames here. Mobility will be slow, dangerous—but surprise will be our shield."*

Ptolemy nodded. *"The downstream shallow can hold a fraction of our force. It can serve as a staging ground or desperate escape—but never the main assault."*

Seleucus frowned. *"Horses will struggle. We must send light cavalry first, trained to swim if need be, to secure the far bank."*

Perdiccas added, *"Engineering teams must work swiftly to prepare the crossing. We have weeks held in the monsoon's grasp. Every moment counts."*

As strategies spun into plans, Alexander's appetite for action grew. The waiting—the torment of stasis—would soon break.

"We march as soon as these preparations suit," he declared. "The river will not claim our fate by patience."

Outside, the swollen Hydaspes mocked his resolve, roaring and churning, a primordial judge waiting to witness the reckoning of kings.

But inside the tent, the Macedonian war council burned with renewed purpose.

The future now hinged upon fragile timbers and the iron will of men who dared cross the unyielding river.

Chapter 25: Shadows and Strategy on the Hydaspes

The rain-soaked jungle exhaled wet and heavy under the weight of monsoon thunder, its thick canopy shielding the murmurs of a restless war camp. Weeks had passed in tense standoff along the swollen banks of the Hydaspes River, yet within Alexander's mind, the gears of destiny turned with fresh clarity. The scouts' reports, though marked by the ferocity of the river's currents and the watchful eyes of Porus's army, had revealed a thread of hope—frail, dangerous, but tangible.

Porus's soldiers observed with hawk-like vigilance, their myriad eyes tracking every ripple of movement on the opposite bank. Distance and storm-clouds blurred the true intentions behind the Macedonian stirrings, but Alexander knew an enemy could never comprehend fully what one concealed beneath shadow and silence. It was this veil—woven from distance, rain, and carefully staged deception—that would become the loom for his cunning plan.
Summoned beneath a heavy, silk-draped tent, Alexander's generals gathered, faces sharp, muscles taut with anticipation. The great commander's voice broke the quiet.
"Long have we waited," Alexander began, gaze steady, *"and long have we been shadowed by eyes unblinking. Yet those eyes see only what we show—never what we choose to hide."*
Unfolding the scouts' maps and reports, he traced his finger along the river's snaking course. *"Upstream lies our path—a narrow channel skirted by a wooded island. Here, horses and men may cross with stealth and speed. Here, I will lead a division and seize the far bank."*

He paused, tension balancing on every syllable.
"Downstream, another force will cross, threatening Porus's line and dividing his attention. To draw eyes and arms away from these true strikes, smaller detachments—no more than five hundred men each—will stage attacks and make crossing attempts, feints to bait and bewilder."
Heads nodded in quiet accord, the generals' resolve matching their king's.
Orders flew swift as darkened swallows through camp, and the masquerade began. Small forces disappeared into the jungle's wet green to construct rafts and repair hastily built boats. Archers took positions and loosed volleys against Porus's distant sentinels, protecting the boat-builders' labor with well-aimed storms of arrows. The noise and frantic activity mimicked the chaos of real battle preparations.
Across the river, Porus's scouts reported these movements with urgency. The seasoned king sent troops in response—swift, determined, believing these assaults born of a desperate foe eager to cross. He moved his forces along the riverbank in waves, chasing shadows, fighting skirmishes that thinned his ranks.
Porus conceived Alexander's actions as the erratic outbursts of an army burdened by time and fever, desperate to force a crossing before the monsoon worsened. But he failed to pierce the veil of deception—the true force lingered upstream, gathering strength.
As more Macedonian troops built visible tension at feint points, Porus stretched his forces ever thinner, placing men where Alexander wanted them—away from the coming storm of his main divisions. Battles flared along the river, and blood mourned both sides, but Alexander's true plan was safeguarded by this tempest of misdirection.
In the shadowed groves upstream, Alexander's battle-hardened forces prepared silently, shielded by jungle and storm. The conduit of marshaled thunder was ready to

surge—the island between river forks held promise as both shield and springboard.
Patience, guile, and disciplined bravery took hold where rage might have failed. Alexander's lattice of deception had pulled the enemy's teeth, leaving Porus vulnerable to the coming strike.
The stage was set for history.
The river—violent, merciless, yet defied—waited to become the gateway of the empire.

Chapter 26: The Feints and the Forging of a Crossing

The humid jungle air weighed heavy, washed in endless rain and alive with the restless murmur of the swollen Hydaspes. Along its banks, Alexander's soldiers labored feverishly, working to bring wood and bamboo to the river's edge. Under a deluge of raindrops and occasional thunder cracks, they built rafts and boats with rough-hewn logs lashed tightly, timber frames patched with woven reeds. Their desperate hands hammered, tied, and shaped instruments of river passage.

Meanwhile, arrows arced from shadowy groves, loosed by soldiers tasked with guarding this fragile flotilla. They formed a protective veil around the boat-builders, fending off Porus's vigilant skirmishers who prowled the opposite shore. The clashing of bowstrings and the thudding of hammer strokes created a discordant symphony in the storm's midst. But fortune, as ever, bore no certainty in war.
One overzealous commander, eager to seize glory, pushed forward prematurely. Gathering thirty men, he launched a

small raft, held by ropes and weighted to keep it steady against the river's rapid pulse. The attempt was bold but ill-fated. Porus's archers spotted the movement and rained arrows upon the fragile craft. Chaos struck: some Macedonians fell to the river, others sank beneath the ruthless current, dragged away like driftwood beneath the surging waters.

The loss was tragic yet measured—small in number, but heavy in spirit.

Yet from this sacrifice sprang a critical advantage. Porus, perceiving the determined attempts and brave losses, believed the Macedonians to be desperate, risking much to force their passage. His thoughts narrowed—if these men would throw themselves so fiercely against the river's wrath, surely the main force must be ready to cross soon.

Emboldened by this impression, Porus doubled his efforts along the riverbank, dispatching more troops to confront the scattered feints, further thinning his defensive lines.

Alexander, ever watchful, read his enemy well. The enemy was busy, drawn into the web of false advances.

Now was the moment to strike the true chord.

The great king summoned his generals with quiet urgency, entrusting the deceptive efforts wholly to his capable officers and ordering them to maintain the feints—showing boldness where needed, retreating tactfully when pressed—to keep Porus occupied. Alexander himself prepared to lead the main division upstream, where the river split around a wooded island, a place that promised concealment and advantage. Sending a substantial contingent downstream as well, he aimed to stretch Porus's attention to breaking point.

The journey upstream spanned nearly twenty-five miles—a treacherous passage through dense jungle and treacherous terrain. Supplies had been meticulously gathered: cavalry mounts, weapons, tents, and tools for bridging the river's unpredictability.

General Hephaestion and other commanders worked tirelessly to hold and provoke Porus's forces at the feint points downstream, weaving illusions of imminent crossing and engaging in small skirmishes to distract and delay.
After two arduous days traversing rainforest and uneven trails, Alexander arrived at the hidden ford—where the river's anger seemed slightly tempered by the river island's protective arms.
Here, the crossing would demand more than mere courage.
As night fell, Macedonian forces camped quietly on the island's forested banks. The water before them ran deep and merciless, threatening to sweep away horses and men alike.
Ingenious measures were set in motion: ropes were tied to trees and large stones on both banks to secure horses and rafts. The soldiers constructed narrow, makeshift bridges from bamboo and woven ropes, fragile spans that swayed above the churning river.
The task was monumental—and dangerous.
Through painstaking effort, the Macedonian vanguard managed to ferry half their force across by dusk.
On the other side, they set up camp carefully among dense foliage, readying themselves for the final day of crossing and battle to come.
Meanwhile, downstream, another group of Alexander's troops found a natural stone ford, localized between jagged banks where the waters lingered shallowly. They used fallen branches lashed together to stabilize the crossing, sending men carefully in staggered waves to avoid collapse. Camp was established before dawn, silent but alert, preparing for a sudden advance on Porus's flank.
Despite signs that their plans were becoming known, Alexander understood well the burden he imposed on Porus's decisions—either to divide his strength to meet multiple threats or to remain resolutely defensive and risk being overwhelmed piecemeal.
Both choices played into Macedonian hands.

As rafts floated, boats were pushed into currents, and soldiers staggered under load across shaky bamboo bridges, the great play of shadow and steel unfolded.
The deep, roaring Hydaspes stood as both challenge and ally, its relentless current symbolic of the storm about to break over ancient battlegrounds.
Alexander's crossing was no mere act of strength; it was a symphony of careful misdirection, relentless will, and daring innovation.
The final reckoning awaited beyond the river's embrace.

Chapter 27: Signal Fires and The Gathering Storm

Suspicion hung over Porus's camp like the rain-soaked monsoon clouds clustering above the mighty Hydaspes. For weeks, the riverbank had been a theater of chaos—Greek soldiers launching feints, building boats, testing crossings in waves, all while Porus's defenders chased each threat. Yet now, the rhythm of battle faltered.

Porus stood in his command pavilion, ringed by his chief lieutenants. The latest reports from the far banks brought little comfort: small Greek units gathered, split, vanished into jungle, only to reappear downriver building new rafts or kindling another diversionary skirmish. But then the feints slowed and a strange quiet fell. Porus—his brow furrowed—aired his doubts aloud.
"These attacks," he mused, *"they bleed us, yes, but I fear their true aim is distraction. Alexander is planning something greater."*

His chiefs agreed. For days, manpower had been spent battling shadows, stretching defenses thin. Now, Porus decreed that no more soldiers would be wasted chasing ghosts. Instead, he ordered his army's main body to fortify the center, rallying strength for whatever storm was coming.

As Porus's forces consolidated, the Greeks understood their subterfuge had been pierced. But Alexander had prepared for just this—his commanders, experienced in the subtle languages of war, lit signal torches that night. The fires crackled into the mist, visible for miles, a coded message to all Macedonian detachments: The moment had come.

On both sides of the great river, leaders saw the flames and knew. Alexander's attack was about to begin.

Porus summoned his war council late into the damp night. Maps were set, scouts dispatched, possibilities debated—where would Alexander strike? From the jungle upstream, from the feint positions near the center, or in a bold sweep from downstream? Each scenario held dangers, but none seemed certain. The Indian chiefs argued, strategized, and prayed with every hour, the suspense grew.

Greek encampments, meanwhile, hummed with focused energy. Alexander, ever patient and calculating, issued his final orders. Bridges of bamboo and rope were built between the island and shore. Cavalrymen steadied nervous horses as engineers secured anchor lines. Spears and shields were checked one last time in the moonlight. Even the downstream detachments began their careful maneuvers, ensuring all was set for a synchronized assault.

Alexander, wary of spies or villagers betraying his surprise, gave stern orders: no mercy for those who might slip word to Porus's camp. Stealth and secrecy became sacred duties. Every man in the Macedonian host understood—the king wished this attack to be his masterstroke, the blow that would break Porus and win the spoils to reward his restless troops.

For two days and nights, the Greeks advanced, masked by jungle, distance, and the remnants of the storm. Their progress, though slow, was relentless. At every turn, Alexander made sure confusion reigned—fires, march sounds, messengers darting between camp and river—all designed to obscure the true direction of attack.

Porus, for his part, maintained his center, sending trusted commanders to probe the river's edges but keeping his elephants and chariots ready for movement in any direction. Yet unease gnawed at the defenders. Rumor raced through the Paurava ranks: Alexander was coming, but none knew when or how.

Finally, on the eve of the battle, all suspense reached its breaking point. Porus watched the jungle anxiously, aware his adversary's patience was legendary, his cunning peerless. Within Alexander's lines, torches guttered as final signals were exchanged. Horses whinnied low, soldiers gripped shields and swords, and the commanders steeled themselves. There would be no more waiting. Both armies, hearts pounding with dread and hope, moved as one mighty tide toward the inevitable clash.

The fate of two kings, two worlds, and the mighty Hydaspes itself hung upon the dawn.

Chapter 28: The Advance to Confrontation

The crossing was complete. Alexander's vanguard, exhausted but triumphant, had forded the Hydaspes from the island's muddy banks, using a latticework of rope bridges, hastily lashed bamboo span, and the raw strength of determined men. Simultaneously, his other division had made it across from the downstream ford, each contingent shielding its movements with secrecy and ruthlessness—no word of their approach allowed to slip into the forests and villages between them and Porus's camp.

Now—spread out across the lush, rain-soaked river plain—the Macedonian phalanxes gathered in orderly columns, cavalry reformed and scouts raced forward under the mottled sky. The great gamble had paid off; the river, which Porus had deemed an impregnable defense, lay behind them.

Within Porus's war pavilion, the tension was palpable. Scouts, installed just a half-day's ride from the outskirts, raced back with alarming news: not only had the Greeks managed the impossible crossing, they were advancing fast, both from the upper and lower banks. Porus, stunned by Alexander's endurance and the audacity of the maneuver, convened his command council for an emergency meet.

The discussion was desperate. Should they divide their force? Attempt a direct charge? Porus argued for personal leadership at the front—honor dictating that kings must face the invader head-on. Yet the old sage, Rajaguru, reminded the gathering that Porus was needed at the center, anchoring the morale and strategic resistance of his people. The kingdom itself needed its king, should the enemy break through.

Rajaguru's wisdom won out. Veerabhalla, renowned for his battlefield instincts, was sent to meet the onrushing Greeks, while Porus remained behind, tasked with fortifying the main camp and readying the massive army for the true confrontation. *"We will use what the land gives us,"* Rajaguru advised. *"These Greeks do not know the mud, the trees, the hidden streams. Make the river's far bank their enemy as much as our swords."*

Veerabhalla, commander of 6,000 seasoned warriors—archers, horsemen, and heavy infantry—set out under the flag of resistance, the pounding of hooves and footfalls echoing through the morning mist. The archers, quick-footed and keen-eyed, deployed forward in staggered ranks; the cavalry rode behind, ready for lightning charges; and the infantry braced themselves to stand against the tide that Alexander would bring.

Alexander, meanwhile, pressed on with speed. His men covered ground at a desperate pace, fueled by the knowledge that surprise was their greatest asset and time their greatest enemy. The drumbeat of progress rang through the jungle as messengers relayed orders to keep the ranks tight, to silence any straggler who might give up the plan, and to prepare for imminent battle.
Neither side fully knew what waited in the forested no-man's-land between them. Alexander, ever calculating, did not expect a full Indian army to meet him so soon; Veerabhalla, for his part, knew that even if faced alone, he must delay the Greeks as long as possible for Porus's main force to settle and prepare.

By late afternoon, Veerabhalla's advanced scouts had established a skirmish line in the tangled undergrowth near the central road. Paurava archers began firing probing shots into the bush—testing for Greek positions, seeking signs of movement or reply. Alexander's own scouts flanked these positions, reporting the landscape: marshes here, clearings there, a wide swath of churned mud where elephants had trained.

The vanguard of both armies was less than a day's march apart.
Both leaders sensed the tension in the air. Alexander felt the weight of destiny, knowing that this would be the first real clash—a test of steel, skill, and speed. Veerabhalla readied his men, drawing them in tight with whispered commands, promising them honor if they held the line.
In Porus's camp, the king moved through his soldiers' ranks, giving words of encouragement, helping engineers fortify trenches and palisades. Rajaguru circulated, blessing warriors and uttering ancient prayers for strength and endurance.

As dusk settled, the Macedonian army halted, building fires low and keeping voices hushed. Horses grazed, men tightened their belts, and bared blades were sharpened. Alexander convened his generals underneath a broad canopy, laying out the morning's attack in detail, reminding each officer of terrain traps and Indian tactics.

On the Indian side, Veerabhalla's men did not sleep. Small patrols probed forward, reporting the shimmer of torches and the quiet movement of cavalry in the Greek camp. The air hummed with anticipation—every insect and every blade of grass seemed to wait for the thunder to break.
And so night fell: two armies, both masterpieces of discipline, resolve, and cunning, poised in the jungles and river plains. The Greeks had crossed the impossible Hydaspes; the Indians braced for the charge. Honor, vengeance, and fate were to be determined at dawn.

Chapter 29: Ghosts Beneath the Canopy

Dawn broke in veils of mist, soft and cool over the forests fringing the Hydaspes. The river itself, no longer a barrier but a silent accomplice, lay behind both advancing Greek columns and the main force of Veerabhalla's defenders. The Greeks who'd crossed overnight from the other bank left a force in reserve before hastening to join the central march—Alexander wanted the weight of his army brought to bear swiftly on Porus, to preserve momentum and the shock of surprise.

Within the Paurava camp, uncertainty stewed. Porus, Rajaguru, and their generals convened in a dim-lit council tent as runners brought word from forested spies—the Greek host was moving with rare discipline, avoiding all villages, silencing anyone who witnessed their passing. The enemy was less than two days away and the flanking column was closer still, but Porus had not deployed any major resistance along their expected route, hoping to lure them into deeper forest.

Rajaguru's strategy was now the only shield against disaster. He ordered a full third of his archers—thousands of men—to vanish into the leafy shadows, each given strict instructions for silence and patience. Their bows and arrows, oiled and fletched, blended into the green; at a word from Porus, they would become the sky's vengeance, unleashing an arrow storm on the unaware Greek lines. War elephants—normally unwieldy on open plains—had been trained in maneuvering through jungle, their mahouts masters at stealth. Only at the last moment would the enemy see these forest giants, thundering from concealment at flank and rear, raising chaos where order seemed assured.

Foot soldiers, cavalry, and more elephants were assigned to flexible flanks, each unit small enough to vanish among trees yet large enough to strike hard—Rajaguru knew that speed and surprise, native to the land, would be Paurava's best answer to phalanx discipline.

Porus called together his junior officers, imparting his will. *"We fight as sons of this soil, not as prey of a plain. Let Alexander learn every shadow here holds death."* The king and Rajaguru spent the remaining hours reinforcing trenches with logs, sharpening stakes, and distributing painted banners along hidden paths, signals for units to coordinate ambushes at need.

Meanwhile, Veerabhalla moved out at pace. His troops covered ground as if born in the brush—archers ghosted forward, cavalry swept through clearings, and scouts reported intact ahead and to flank. The morning was thick with anticipation; they knew the Greeks advanced in disciplined files, but the forest negated their numbers. At any moment, the clash would begin.

Across the river, Alexander marshaled his warriors, officers counting heads and giving stern orders—maintain formation, silence all noise, preserve the element of surprise. Yet as the forest closed in, even the boldest Macedonians felt unease. The ground was slick, visibility patchy, every tree a possible hiding place for a Paurava archer.

Both armies marched. Veerabhalla's force, now close enough to sense the enemy's torches and distant, low voices, readied for the imminent faceoff. Alexander and his generals grimly checked gear, adjusted horses, and made final plans for the attack most had dreamed of.

Unseen, the forest watched. Porus and Rajaguru waited for the signal—the one that would call their archers from shadow and unleash the deadly rain.

As the Greek and Indian vanguards converged—each moving at speed, each trusting in discipline and cunning—the hydaspes campaign reached its boiling point.

The jungle itself seemed to tremble—knowing that within its depths, the fates of kings and empires were about to be decided by the ghosts beneath the canopy.

Chapter 30: Clash of Titans

Veerabhalla stood beneath the heavy canopy, the rain from the previous night still clinging to the leaves above. Rajaguru's voice echoed relentlessly in his mind, a constant reminder of his duty: resist Alexander's advance and buy time for the main army to prepare. He knew the battle would not be won here, but retreat only when forced—when his forces were overwhelmed—would preserve his men for the decisive fight to come. This was war as strategy, as much about endurance and study as about valor.

He made this clear to his soldiers. *"Hold firm—fight as if for your lives. Watch Alexander closely. Learn his tactics, remember his moves. We retreat only when the time is right."* Both armies moved with silent urgency. A signal was given, lanterns flickered, and within moments, the two enormous forces thundered toward each other across the soaked earth.

At the front, the soldiers gripped their long spears like extensions of their own bodies, pushing forward with a deadly, synchronized force honed through the ferocity of battle. The sharp points found their marks relentlessly—piercing through shields, meeting flesh with sickening thuds, tearing into sinew and bone amidst a chaos swirling in red and steel. Men screamed, fell, and surged as lines buckled and pressed again, a never-ending tide of violence.

High above, the air crackled with tension as archers commanded the sky. Greek bowmen loosed volleys with lethal precision, each arrow thudding into a shield or finding a mortal chink. Paurava archers perched motionless in the towering trees—hidden sentinels armed with shafts dipped in venomous poison—awaited their command, their presence blending perfectly with the canopy's shadows.

Horses reared and faltered, hooves stomping erratically as arrows found their throats or legs. Many beasts fell, taking riders with them in crashes of flesh and wood. Foot soldiers pressed on, slicing mercilessly at dismounted foes—murder woven into every stroke of a sword.

Amidst this furious melee, a Greek commander, smaller in stature yet formidable, ducked past the chaos. Reckless in his charge, he sought to strike a blow against Veerabhalla himself. But fate had other designs. From behind, an Indian soldier lifted his bow with lightning reflexes, drawing the string taut to release a single, fatal arrow. The shaft pierced through the back of the commander's skull, piercing from the base of the head and exiting gruesomely through his mouth as he pitched forward in a silent, deadly arc.

Nearby, some soldiers who lost swords adapted with grim resilience, turning their heavy shields into bludgeoning weapons, hacking at enemies who dared close. The clash of metal against metal echoed against the roar of battle, mingling with cries of pain, shouts of encouragement, and the desperate prayers of warriors locked in mortal combat.

The Greeks fought as veterans of battered foreign lands, their movements a harsh dance of practiced routines, their bodies conditioned by endless campaigns. The Paurava, though fewer in battle experience, wielded the raw vigor of men defending their homeland, adapting rapidly in the cauldron of war, and refusing to yield an inch of ground.

Veerabhalla rode with murderous grace, his double-edged sword a blur as he cut through enemy ranks. His eyes flickered across the battlefield, reading the Greek formations, noting weaknesses and timing

In the distance, Veerabhalla glimpsed a figure atop a striking black steed—Alexander, astride Bucephalus, weaving through the battlefield like a living storm. The mighty horse moved as if driven by lightning itself, unhindered by the chaos beneath its hooves. Alexander's presence was Herculean, a towering man with blond-reddish hair and a beard like a lion's mane, radiating power and fearlessness.

Recognition struck Veerabhalla like a bolt. Though this was his first sight of the conqueror, Alexander's stature and aura marked him instantly.

Spurred, Veerabhalla urged his horse forward, charging toward the Macedonian king.

Blood flowed freely. Both sides suffered grievous losses; Veerabhalla's ranks thinned faster under the harsh discipline and battle-hardened Greeks. Even so, he pressed on. Signaling his captains mid-charge, he ordered preparations for retreat—to preserve what was left and ensure the king had time.

The two warriors met in a thunderous clash that echoed across the blood-soaked ground. Veerabhalla, fierce and unyielding, launched a sudden, powerful lunge. The steel glinted like lightning as his sword sliced through the air, forcing Alexander to shield and twist beneath the assault. Their horses reared and flicked their tails wildly, both beasts stumbling—then mid-charge, the riders toppled unceremoniously to the ground.

Alexander landed with the grace of a seasoned warrior, rolling twice before fluidly springing to his feet. His eyes flashed with the fire of challenge, burning with the spirit of conquest. Veerabhalla rose too, muscles coiled and ready, dripping with sweat and grime—two warriors molded by relentless struggle, equal in stature and strength, tempered by the cruel forge of war.

They circled warily, each step measured and deliberate. Their swords soon sang a metallic symphony—clangs of bold strokes, fierce parries, and the sharp ring of steel reverberating through the battlefield's din. Their movements were poetry wrought of battle, each exchanging blows not just of weapon but of will.

For the first time, Alexander felt the thrill of true opposition—the exhilarating apprehension of a worthy adversary who could match his skill and spirit. The Paurava commander was no mere warrior but a rival equal, posing a challenge that ignited Alexander's respect.

Their deadly dance captivated onlookers—their swords striking with a rhythm so precise and symmetrical that it seemed less war than a choreographed duel. Each clash produced sparks and reverberated like thunder. The uneasy silence around the combatants spoke volumes of the breathless awe evoked by their fight.

Veerabhalla's every strike was met with an equally determined parry, his footwork mirroring Alexander's with calculated precision. Their steel slid against steel, neither yielding ground nor advantage. The duel was a contest of both physical might and mental fortitude.

But war's cruel necessity loomed. Veerabhalla's captains, their voices strained and quick, signaled the time had come for withdrawal. He understood the grim duty: retreat now to preserve lives and regroup with the main force, even if his fierce warrior's heart rebelled at the thought of turning away from battle.

With a reluctant gesture, Veerabhalla signaled his troops. The soldiers executed a careful, shield-protected retreat as their leader mounted a fresh horse, helped by a steadfast captain—a brother in arms ensuring the survival of their cause.

Alexander, watching this, was struck by Veerabhalla's courage, loyalty, and tactical acumen. Within him grew an appreciation for the warrior's mind that opposed him—a knowledge that would enrich the battles still to come.

The toll was terrible. Over half the Paurava soldiers lay dead; Greek losses tallied around two thousand. But the delay had been bought. Porus's main army now had precious time to prepare for the battle to come.

Chapter 31: Blood and Shadows Before the Storm

Veerabhalla's retreat back was marked by silence more telling than the roar of battle—a silence that spoke of loss but also of purpose fulfilled. Alexander, battered and bruised, made no attempt to pursue the withdrawing Paurava forces. His own ranks had suffered heavy casualties; hundreds lay wounded and broken. The Macedonian king ordered a halt, commanding his soldiers to rest and tend to their dying as twilight descended. Thus, the night embraced both victors and vanquished.

Veerabhalla, though reluctant to withdraw, obeyed the sage counsel of Rajaguru. He understood well that a true victory was often won through patience and strategy, that some battles must be lost to win the war.Within his heart, respect had grown for Alexander's unmatched valor. The Greek's strength was no mere legend; it was steel and blood in motion, a force that had challenged Veerabhalla's warriors to their limits.

As dusk fell on the eve of battle, Rajaguru gathered his trusted commanders beneath the canopy of the vast forest bordering the battlefield. The air was heavy with the scent of damp earth and simmering tension. Before the first arrow was loosed or any blade drawn, the strategist's mind was already many steps ahead, weaving a web of plans that leveraged both the landscape and the enemy's expectations.

"The Greeks believe they face our full might at the front," Rajaguru mused, tracing the lines of the riverbanks and forest

with a slender finger. *"They see the downstream army, clustered and ready, but that is but a fraction—our bait, our mirror to their own tactics."*
His voice was steady, voice low like the hiss of winds through the trees. *"I shall divide our forces to confuse and overwhelm. Ten thousand will stand headlong against the Greeks downstream, clear and visible—a fortress of men meant to draw their eyes and steel."*
Then, his eyes brightened with calculated purpose. *"While they fixate there, flanks shall slip like shadows from the forest—silent as the monsoon mists that cloak these lands. These warriors will strike where the enemy's courage wavers, ripping muscle and nerve with unexpected fury."*
He motioned toward the towering trees lining the battlefield. *"Thousands of archers will ascend into the canopy—masters of patience and precision. Camouflaged among leaves and branches far above the ground, their arrows sharpened and some dipped in potent poison, will wait for the signal to unleash a storm—arrows like a deadly monsoon falling upon Alexander's troops."*
The archers would blend so perfectly they would appear as part of the forest itself—silent watchers whose presence would turn the tides in an instant.
Rajaguru's command was meticulous: *"The front line holds. It will fix the Greeks in place, forcing them to commit their forces. When confusion ripples through their ranks, the forest will come alive with our hidden flanks. The ambush will be swift and brutal. The enemy will find they fight not only as men, but against an entire wilderness."*
The commanders listened intently, the scale and subtlety of the plan unfolding like a piece of sacred scripture. Rajaguru paused, looking toward the horizon where the first lamps of the Greek camp began to twinkle.
"Tomorrow, this land will defend itself. Let Alexander's men learn that these jungles are no mere backdrop for war—they are a weapon."

A hushed reverence fell over the group as the weight of what was to come settled like a thick fog. Tomorrow, the battle would be more than clash of steel—it would be a contest of shadows, will, and death beneath the monsoon skies. Porus, dressed in gleaming armor and wielding a sword ancient and sharp enough to cleave thick tree trunks, strode among the gathered warriors. His eyes burned with fierce determination. The weight of the forthcoming conflict pressed upon all.Beside him, Rajaguru chanted sacred verses, invoking the favor of gods and ancestors. *"This battle," he intoned,* " is no mere contest of arms but a sacred yajña. Its fire shall forge the spirit of Bharat for generations to come."

The waters of the Hydaspes shimmered crimson from the upstream clash fought so fiercely. The river, ancient witness to countless wars, seemed to mourn the coming slaughter even as it awaited the final, decisive storm.In the gathering twilight, the armies braced for combat that promised no quarter—no more deception, no more waiting. Only raw, brutal force would decide the fate of kingdoms and kings.

As the sky darkened, clouds gathered, heavy and foreboding, as if nature itself knew the world was poised on the brink of an unforgettable war.

Chapter 32: The Gathering Storm of Battle

The dense jungle around the swollen Hydes now echoed with the whispered prayers and subdued whistles of thousands of warriors. The forces of Paurava had settled into their finalized positions, each soldier charged with a destiny forged in the blood and sweat of preparation. Every trap was hidden beneath moss and vine; every formation folded seamlessly into the tangled forest and muddy plains.

Porus and Rajguru stood atop an ancient outcrop, the vantage offering a panoramic view of the battlefield—a patchwork of shifting shadows and glinting steel. The predators watched, poised and patient.

"The day that has haunted our twilight approaches," Rajguru murmured, lips moving in sacred chant.

Porus, clad in armor that shimmered like the river itself, gripped his legendary sword. *"We transform attack into resistance," he declared. "Let the invader see how a people born of earth can bite like its granite."*

As night deepened, the Greek vanguard from downstream reached the plains, making camp mere miles from Paurava's main encampment. The seasoned commander leading them was a proven veteran of Macedon's past campaigns in Bactria—a lion among men whose voice carried unquestioned authority. His soldiers revered him, his strategy will and decisiveness inspiring unwavering loyalty.

The surrounding forest was alive with movement. Paurava scouts slipped silently through the underbrush, positioning themselves far beyond typical watchlines. Rajguru's orders were clear: patience and precision were paramount. The moment the horn sounded, ambush and chaos would rend the opposing ranks.

In the darkness, Rajguru methodically split the army into multiple columns and flanking parties. Some were assigned the frontal assault—to maintain the illusion that the entire force awaited before the Greeks. This vanguard, a mix of foot soldiers and hardened spearmen, stood ready to engage head-on.

Elsewhere, small units coveted the whispering forest, their approach masked by careful camouflage and familiarity with every tree and creek. The archers scaled towering limbs, ready to release arrows laden with deadly poison the moment battle exploded.

Porus's warriors, though less experienced, fought with fierce determination. The terrain was their ally, the shadows their shield. They ran light and fast, striking quick and vanishing like wraiths amidst the green.

At dawn, Porus performed his war rites. Flames crackled deep in the night, the scent of burning sandalwood rising skyward mingled with the earthy musk of fresh blood and rain. Warriors laid out their weapons, adjusting the leather straps, polishing the steel edges. The king donned his armor, which clanked a steady, beautiful rhythm, a prelude to the coming storm.

"The sword I carry can cleave mountains, " Porus vowed, sliding the ancient blade into his grip. *"But this day, it shall carve history anew."*

Rajguru chanted to the gods of battlefield and forest, seeking blessings and fortitude, their voices blending with the dirge of cicadas and the roiling winds that swept through the canopy.

Morning broke with a leaden sky. The armies emerged from their cover, dawn breath stirred the air heavy with anticipation and iron.

Both sides formed their battle lines with care—steel clashing gently in practice, horses stamping, arrows nocked. The

battlefield was a living canvas, painted first with the gleam of armor, then with the blood of men.
Captains shouted orders, horns sounded, and the silence shattered with the thunder of thousands of feet and hooves.

The earth trembled under the thunderous charge as the two armies collided in a violent embrace. The front ranks wielded long spears that thrust and stabbed like the teeth of a great beast, each finding its mark piercing armor and flesh alike. The Macedonian phalanx, trained to act as a single living wall of stabbing sarissas, pressed forward relentlessly, forcing the Paurava foot soldiers into a desperate and brutal contest of endurance.

Around them, archers loosed a storm of arrows, thickening the air with deadly intent. Greek archers perched behind their ranks released shafts that whistled and clanged against Indian shields. In turn, Paurava archers, hidden atop towering trees, rained arrows down like a merciless monsoon on the Macedonian ranks. Many men raised their shields just in time, others crumpled and fell, crimson silently blossoming across the soaked battlefield.
Horses reared and stumbled under the hail of arrows—black beasts that bolted wildly or crashed onto the bloodied ground, pinning soldiers beneath their massive bodies. Quick-footed infantry used the chaos of horse falls to strike lethal blows, severing limbs and cleaving heads.
One Macedonian commander, slight and fierce, darted forward through the melee, only to face a deadly fate: a Paurava soldier, steady and silent amidst the frenzy, loosed an arrow that found its cruel mark just behind the commander's helmet. The shaft pierced through the soft spot under his skull, emerging grotesquely through his mouth. The commander pitched forward, eyes wide in frozen shock, collapsing upon his fallen steed.

In the midst of ebbing waves of battle, Rajguru, eyes sharp as a hawk's, sensed an opening. Timing was everything. With a swift gesture, he commanded two concealed flanks—units that had blended into the forest and underbrush—to surge forward.

Like thunder rolling from the treetops, these flanks crashed into the Macedonian sides with brutal ferocity. The Greeks, momentarily caught off guard, faltered, their disciplined lines wavering amidst a growing tide of confusion. Arrows and blades from hidden foes found vulnerable points, disrupting tightly held spear formations.

Finding their formation threatened, Greek commanders acted swiftly. Shouting orders, they reorganized, deploying reserve troops to strengthen the faltering flanks. Soldiers fell into formation, forming secondary lines to blunt the surprise strike and regain control.

But Rajguru's strategic mind was relentless. Seizing the defenders' momentary distraction, he unleashed yet another pair of flanking units from the forest's depths. These reinforcements struck the rear and flanks of the Macedonian forces, sewing chaos and threatening encirclement.

The Greeks, overwhelmed by attacks at multiple points, struggled to maintain cohesion. The battlefield was no longer a clash of two lines but a roiling, twisting map of combat and counterattack that led Greeks to fall.

As the battle smoke slowly lifted and the final echoes of clashing swords faded, the Paurava warriors set about the solemn task of gathering their fallen foes. The battlefield was a scarred and sullen place — bloodied earth, broken spears, shattered shields, and scattered bodies forming a grievous mosaic of war's toll. The Paurava soldiers, fierce in their valor, showed great respect in the aftermath: carefully and reverently collecting the dead Greeks, arranging their bodies in ordered ranks as if to restore their dignity even in death.

Porus, standing among his commanders and priests, surveyed the scene with a measured eye. Yet a question sat heavily upon his mind—unspoken but ever-present. They had never witnessed the funeral customs of these foreign invaders. Several Paurava nobles and Rajaguru conferred in whispered tones. The rites, the mourning customs, the way to honor the dead were strange to their eyes and hearts.
"This land knows no such rites," one elder murmured .
"And we have no knowledge of how to send these warriors to their ancestors' rest."
Another replied gravely, *"The ways must be honored, lest the spirits unrest and bring ill omen."*
Porus inclined his head, wisdom guiding him. *"We shall await the arrival of Alexander. Let him come, and show honor to his dead in the manner of his people. This is a sign of respect, and perhaps a bridge between two worlds."*
Thus, the Paurava king decreed that no further rites would be performed until Alexander appeared. They would give the Macedonian king the time and dignity to perform the necessary ceremonies, fostering honor even amidst enmity.

Veerabhalla who came from the battle with Alexander joined with rajaguru and porus , despite his central role in delaying the enemy, bore deep sorrow for his losses. In the shadowed council tent, he confessed his grief to Porus and Rajguru.
"War demands sacrifice," Rajguru consoled softly. *"The brave embrace it for the greater good. Your honor is in your wisdom, not just valor."*

Gathered close, Veerabhalla shared with the king and commander the invaluable insights gained from observing Alexander's tactics—a fierce, cunning mind, adaptable and relentless.

With new knowledge and renewed determination, Porus and his advisers set about their next maneuvers, preparing for the war's ultimate culmination.

Chapter 33 – The Calm Before the Storm

The rout of Alexander's downstream army had sent ripples across Aryavarta. For the first time, the people of Paurava, most of whom had lived quiet lives of farming, trade, or minor skirmishes between lords, felt the intoxicating fire of victory. Their spirits grew iron-strong. This was no longer a border clash or raid—it was destiny itself, unfolding before their eyes.

From Veerabhalla's information about Macedonian tactics, Porus and the Rajaguru adjusted their strategy. Initially, their plan had been to unleash the elephants in the later stages of the battle. But now, gazing upon the relentless discipline of Alexander's armies, they resolved to bring forward their greatest force at once.

The Rajaguru personally supervised the flanks that stretched on either side of the Hydaspes forest. This time, rows of elephants were embedded into those wings, turning them into towers of thunder, increasing their strength manyfold. The beasts, covered in thick armor, stood like living citadels awaiting command.

On the opposite side, Alexander's forces swelled as reinforcements poured in. More than twenty thousand Greek soldiers converged around him—veterans hardened in campaigns from Thebes to Persia. Alongside them marched the controversial ally of the invader: King Ambhi of Taxila.

Ambhi had no choice. His betrayal of Aryavarta was already sealed; no Indian king would ever aid him again. Only by clutching Alexander's hand could he hope to survive, even if it meant raising his sword against Porus—the king who had once treated him as a brother.

For a full day, Alexander maneuvered his growing host and then positioned camp just far enough to remain safe from Porus' elephants, yet near enough to keep the Paurava under pressure. Porus and the Rajaguru looked eastward at the glittering torches of the Macedonian camp across the plain. They exchanged a silent glance. Both knew: this was the final crucible. Their people, their lands, their honor—all of it rested on the clash of dawn.

Night descended over the Hydaspes. Beneath the vast canopy of stars, two camps—one western, one Indian—beat with the pulse of preparation.

In Alexander's pavilion, a war council gathered. Torchlight danced across bronze armor and scarred faces as commanders bent over maps. Ambhi spoke first.

"These elephants," Ambhi said, his tone edged with unease, *"they are unlike any beast you've faced. They do not flee from sound, nor do they fear fire. Their mahouts have trained them against such tricks. Yet..."* He paused, eyes narrowing. *"...armored or not, fire can still burn. If we cannot make them retreat, let us force them to rage. A panicked elephant turns upon its own. Fire, oil, arrows—they will burn, and then fall upon their own lines."*

Alexander stroked his chin, the torchlight flickering upon his sharp eyes. He nodded slowly. *"Yes. Fire is untamed chaos. Even kings cannot control it. Perhaps neither can Porus."*

They spoke long into the night, devising strategies that combined cavalry speed, phalanx discipline, and cunning tricks against the Indian war beasts.

Meanwhile, across the river, Porus' war tent was heavy with incense and the low hum of hymns. The Rajaguru revealed his insight.

"Ambhi fights alongside the foreigner. He knows our elephants, our discipline, our weaknesses. We cannot underestimate him. But the gods have provided. Do you remember the rain-water pits we dug across our land in past seasons? I have ordered them expanded into great reservoirs. If Ambhi dares to loose fire upon our elephants, the mahouts will drive them not into chaos, but into those waters. The beasts have been trained—fire will enrage them, yes, but only to strike harder after cooling their armor in the pools of Varuna. Their armor may blister, but their hides will not burn."

Porus listened gravely as the Rajaguru's words struck like thunder in the chamber. He imagined the sight of his elephants, their armored tusks gleaming, pouring cool water across their smoldering flanks before storming back into enemy ranks, angrier than before. It brought a fierce grin to his face.

"Alexander faces no beasts of Persia here," Porus finally declared. *"He faces the sons of the five rivers. Tomorrow, he shall learn that this land is not for the taking. This is the land of Purushottama!"*

Throughout the night, both armies readied for the inevitable collision. Torches burned like twin constellations across the plain. Bows were strung, swords sharpened, armor fitted. Elephants rumbled in the darkness, their silhouettes vast against the flicker of flame, while Macedonian horses snorted restlessly, sensing the storm to come.

By dawn, the stage was set. Two worlds—east and west, Aryavarta and Macedon—stood ready beneath the skies of the Hydaspes. The ground itself seemed to tremble, as if the earth awaited the fury about to be unleashed.

Chapter 34 – The Day of the Final War

The long night finally gave way to dawn. A pale mist unrolled across the Hydaspes plain, veiling the earth as if even the gods hesitated to reveal what was about to unfold. The silence before the storm was broken only by the restless hissing of elephants, the stamping of horses, and the heavy drumbeat of war drums echoing from both camps.
Alexander's army stood ready, a living machine of discipline honed by years of conquest. The phalanx stretched across the plain like an unbroken iron wall, its forest of sarissas bristling toward the sky before dipping forward in seamless unison, the spearheads catching the morning sun in a hundred flashes of silver fire. Row upon row of hardened veterans held their lines—men who had marched with Alexander from the burning plains of Persia to the icy slopes of Bactria, men for whom battle was as familiar as bread and water. Their shields overlapped, their armor gleamed, their faces bore the calm ferocity of soldiers who had stood in the shadow of death countless times and emerged alive.

On the flanks, cavalry units pawed at the ground, their horses snorting clouds of vapor into the chill air. These were the pride of Macedon—the Companion Cavalry—noblemen bound by loyalty and glory, their lances sharp and their eyes fixed upon Porus' elephants in the distance. Beyond them, the lighter cavalry contingents—Thracians and Scythians—shifted restlessly, their crescent bows and javelins ready to unleash havoc once the order came.
Behind the front lines, the banners of Macedon rose high, their cloth rippling in the dawn wind. The proud emblem of Zeus' eagle soared upon them, symbol not just of a kingdom, but of Alexander's vision for empire without bounds.

Trumpeters stood at attention, their instruments poised to sound the thunder that would set the army in motion. Every formation was perfectly placed, a dance of order and calculation. The phalanx stood immovable, cavalry flanks glimmered with speed, archers and slingers lurked behind, and reserve lines pressed close—a poem of war written in steel and flesh, crafted by the genius of their young king.

Across the field, Porus' forces unfurled in all their might, a spectacle both terrifying and divine. At the very front stood the war elephants, armored from tusk to tail, great mountains of living flesh and steel. Iron-plated masks covered their foreheads, their curved tusks tipped with gleaming blades. Beneath the golden morning light they appeared less like beasts and more like incarnations of the gods' wrath, summoned to defend Aryavarta. Upon their broad backs sat the mahouts, steady and resolute, murmuring hymns to Varuna and Indra, prayers to guide the beasts through fire, chaos, and slaughter. The elephants raised their trunks and bellowed, the earth itself quaking under their echoed roars.

Behind this wall of giants stood Porus' infantry, row upon row of proud Paurava warriors. They were farmers, herdsmen, hunters, and soldiers alike, their bodies lean and sun-burnished, their eyes full of a fire born not only from duty, but from the desperate love of homeland. Their lines gleamed with an arsenal of war—long spears sharpened to a deadly gleam, curved swords resting in their scabbards, shields painted with the crests of clan and tribe. Archers in hundreds stood ready, their bows strung with care, quivers filled with arrows tipped in iron and poison, each one aimed at the invader's heart.
To the flanks thundered the cavalry of India—kings and vassals who had answered Porus' call. Some bore long bamboo lances, others curved sabres; all sat astride sturdy

horses bred for endurance and ferocity alike. Their banners whipped in the wind: the emblems of allied lords, serpents, lions, and rising suns, adding their color to the Paurava standard that soared high above—a massive banner blazing with the image of the mighty elephant, symbol of strength and sovereignty.

The atmosphere was alive with sound. War drums beat like the heart of Aryavarta itself, their rhythm booming across the plain, shaking both men and beasts into unity. Conch shells blared, their haunting voice echoing toward the heavens, a reminder that this was no ordinary battle—it was a dharmayuddha, a war of righteousness, a defense of sacred motherland.

In their totality they numbered twenty-two thousand—men and beasts together, bound by a single vow. Beside Porus stood his fellow kings, allies who, despite rivalries and grudges of the past, now raised their swords together to hold back the tide of the world.

Before the first command was given, a rider emerged from Porus' camp carrying a letter. Delivered into Alexander's tent, the message bore the unmistakable seal of Paurava. The words were simple yet solemn:

"Many of your brave men fell in the battles with my forces. Their rites have not been performed. I know not the custom of the Greeks, else I would have performed them myself. For honor's sake, if you desire, I shall delay this day of battle until you may complete their final rites."

Alexander read the letter in silence. His eyes darkened with thought, and for a moment, his commanders awaited with tense uncertainty. He remembered his fallen—young men who had walked across deserts, scaled mountains, braved rivers. They deserved the final fires of honor, the prayers of their kin.

He respected Porus deeply in that moment. Few enemies would extend such courtesy at the brink of slaughter. Yet a strategist could not afford to let sentiment rear its head now.

At last, Alexander dipped his pen into ink and wrote his reply:
"King Porus, your respect for the traditions of your enemy, even upon the battlefield, has earned you my admiration. You are indeed a great warrior, worthy of my respect. But I must decline your offer. To delay now would dishonor both my living and my dead, for they march not for rituals of grief but for victory everlasting. When I have won this war, I shall perform their rites with the utmost reverence. I shall also honor your fallen, as you did mine, with equal respect. Let us not delay fate. Let destiny itself decide between us."
The letter was sent back and read aloud in Porus' tent. The Paurava king's brow was stern, but his heart felt the weight of admiration. *Such mastery of one's mind... such control of emotion,* Porus thought. *To accept death as it comes, to deny sorrow in the face of war, this makes him formidable indeed.*
Porus folded the parchment without another word. He lifted his hand high, and his war-drums thundered the signal. The field shuddered at the sound.

On one end of the battlefield, Alexander mounted his beloved Bucephalus, the black stallion that had carried him since youth, a creature as legendary as the king himself. Its coat shimmered like midnight woven with silk, broken only by the radiant white blaze upon its brow—a star that crowned the beast like a divine mark. Bucephalus pawed the earth with proud defiance, nostrils flaring, steam rising in the cold dawn. He was more than a horse; he was Alexander's shadow, bound to him in blood and destiny. Together they had carved empires from the Mediterranean to the Indus, and now they stood ready for their greatest trial. When Alexander leaned forward to stroke its neck, Bucephalus responded with a thunderous neigh, as if he too knew that history itself balanced upon this day.

On the opposite side, Porus swung onto his warhorse, a majestic white stallion that gleamed like moonlight upon fresh snow. The beast's mane rippled like a river of silver, its hooves striking the earth with the cadence of a war drum. This was no ordinary steed—it had carried Porus through years of struggle, from border wars between rival lords to the vast campaigns that now culminated against the greatest conqueror of the West. Adorned with golden fittings and protective armor, the stallion radiated purity and defiance, a living symbol of Aryavarta's resilience. When Porus sat astride the horse, his towering frame clad in shining armor, king and steed merged into a vision of unmatched majesty—an icon his soldiers could rally behind.

Two kings. Two worlds. Two destinies aligned for collision.

The signal horns blared.

The armies lurched forward.

The day of the final war had begun.

Chapter 35 – Clash of Kings

The war had begun.

Both armies lunged forward with such fury that the very earth seemed to tremble. Dust and cries rose into the morning air as steel met flesh, as spears clashed against shields, as war cries echoed like thunder across the plain of Hydaspes. Leading from the front, Porus and Alexander hurled themselves into the fray, each a blazing storm at opposite ends of the battlefield.

Rajaguru had given his first order—a calculated trap. The Paurava front line slackened, pretending to yield ground, luring the phalanx forward deeper into their ranks. The

Greeks, proud of their discipline, pressed hard, believing their heavy wall to be unstoppable. But the Indian warriors, though appearing weaker, held firm with brutal resolve, preparing for the tide to crash upon them.

Porus himself rode at the very heart of the slaughter, a towering colossus upon horseback, his massive frame cloaked in gleaming armor that caught the sun like fire struck upon bronze. To his soldiers, he appeared less a man than a living fortress, unshakable, immovable, the embodiment of their hopes and pride. His white stallion thundered across the churned earth, scattering dust and blood beneath its hooves, carrying its master into the thickest knots of resistance.

In his right hand, Porus wielded a longsword so heavy it might have daunted lesser men, yet in his grip it sang through the air with brutal grace. Each strike fell with the force of a war hammer—helmets split apart, shields shattered, and armored Macedonians fell as if cleaved by a god's hand. Sparks leapt from the impact of ringing steel, but every enemy blade that dared meet his was broken away with overwhelming power.
Yet the king did not rely upon the sword alone. Strapped across his back he bore three, sometimes four spears, balanced and deadly. With a practiced rhythm, Porus reached behind, plucked a spear with lightning speed, and hurled it with devastating precision. Every throw became a storm in itself. The missiles, hurled by his towering strength, screamed through the air and drove into the tightly packed Greek lines, punching through armor, shields, and flesh. In terrifying display, a single throw often skewered three, even four soldiers together, pinning them like a single bundle before they collapsed in lifeless heaps upon the trampled soil. And Porus wasted no time. He surged forward, reclaiming his spears from the fallen, blood-slick wood gripped once

again in his mighty hands, and hurled them anew with relentless fury. His movements were a cycle of destruction—strike with the sword, hurl the spear, reclaim, and strike again—so swift and fluid that the battlefield seemed to obey his rhythm.

Wherever he charged, the enemy lines wavered. The Macedonian phalanx, proud and disciplined, found itself split apart as though the very river of destiny surged through their ranks. Men fell screaming, shields splintered, and the once-ordered wall dissolved in panic wherever Porus advanced. It was as if he was not one man but a hurricane given flesh—an avalanche roaring into the very heart of Alexander's army.

To his soldiers, it was the sight of their king at his mightiest—an undefeatable giant cutting down the enemy as if no force on earth could withstand him. To the Greeks, it was terror incarnate, a vision of an Eastern titan who struck not like a mortal but like Indra himself, hurling thunderbolts into their midst. The closer they came to him, the quicker they died; the farther they tried to retreat, the louder his fury reached them.

Porus carved his legend deeper into the battlefield with every breath, every throw, every swing—painting Hydaspes in blood and glory.

His horse carried him like a whirlwind, hooves pounding storms into the earth as Porus carved furrows of death through the Macedonian lines. But then, above the clamor of swords and the screams of men, a new sound split the air—a thunderous, echoing trumpet cry that silenced even the chaos for an instant. One of Porus' great elephants, sent forward by Rajaguru's foresight, lumbered through the ranks, its armor glinting like dark gold beneath the sun, its tusks capped in sharpened iron. The ground itself trembled at its approach, dust rising in waves as if the earth bowed before its weight.

Porus knew at once the wisdom behind this command. A king on horseback was mighty—but a king upon an elephant was a vision meant for gods. Without hesitation, Porus dismounted and strode toward the colossal beast. Soldiers cheered as they saw their monarch grasp the thick ropes and ascend the towering flank of the animal with the strength of a titan. In moments, he stood high above the battlefield, his silhouette framed against the rising sun.

Now upon his war-elephant, Porus seemed to grow beyond mortal measure. There, amidst smoke and screaming men, he loomed like a mountain of steel, a warrior-king elevated to the stature of the gods of old. From that height, his eyes swept across the battlefield. He beheld the formations, the cracks in the Greek advance, the places where his men faltered, and where they triumphed. The battlefield—the chaos that swallowed ordinary men—was to him a painting, each movement a stroke of destiny, each order he gave shaping history itself.

Armed freshly by Rajaguru's men, Porus now wielded more than a sword and a few spears. Blades glinted in his hands, quivers heavy upon his shoulders, and a great bow carved from seasoned teak rested in his grip. He drew and loosed with the practiced ease of a lifelong warrior, each arrow hissing through the air, piercing helmets, throats, and hearts. No shot was wasted—every shaft claimed an enemy, and the Macedonian advance found itself pierced as though the wrath of the sky itself rained down upon them.

Beneath him, the elephant became the hammer of Varuna. Its tusks, capped in steel, skewered men with sickening force, shattering shields as if they were brittle pottery. When it charged, its massive feet crushed soldiers into the mud, bones splintering beneath the colossal weight. The beast's trumpet cries were shrieks of doom, reverberating deep into the enemy's hearts, scattering courage like chaff in the wind.

Blood splashed across its armor and tusks, painting it into an image of unearthly terror.

Everywhere the elephant rampaged, the Paurava roared in triumph. Soldiers lifted their swords higher, shields firmer, their war cries booming louder across the plain. To see their king elevated upon the mightiest of beasts—hurling arrows, commanding death itself—filled them with something greater than courage. It was as though the gods had descended among them.

Porus raised his bow high, bellowed a cry that rolled like thunder over the battlefield, and his army surged anew with unstoppable ferocity. In that moment, he was no longer just Porus, king of the Pauravas. He was Purushottama, the mighty man, a living vision of war's fury—crushing, commanding, and unbreakable.

Porus raised his hand high, halting his elephant for a breath amid the chaos, and turned his gaze toward the distant ridge where Rajaguru stood with his staff. For one heartbeat, amid the storm of steel and cries of agony, warrior king and spiritual guide met each other's eyes across the sea of death. Gratitude swelled in Porus' chest, and raising his voice like thunder across the plain, he cried:

"He who paints the war with his wisdom—he is the unseen hand behind every victory! Though his blade is equal to a hundred men, greater still is the mind that commands a thousand. Let the master remain in the realm of vision, and we—his disciples, his brushes—shall carve that vision upon flesh and soil!"

The words rolled across the battlefield, carried by the clash of steel and the cry of elephants. Soldiers who heard their king's proclamation roared in approval, their faith in Rajaguru strengthening as though the gods themselves directed his hand. It was not merely strategy they followed—it was dharma, guided by the seer who stood upon the hill.

From his vantage, Rajaguru felt his heart lurch. His old warrior's spirit yearned to leap into the fray, to take up sword and bow, to stand beside his king and fight as he had in his youth. In his mind's eye he could already see himself cutting down Macedonians by the dozens, standing as the equal of mighty men. His knuckles whitened upon his staff as the battle cries reached him.

Yet he knew it was not his place. In this hour, his weapon was not steel, but the vision granted by insight and wisdom. His duty was heavier than bloodshed—it was the shaping of destiny.

Slowly, Rajaguru bowed his head, acknowledging Porus' words. His eyes closed, and he whispered a prayer to the gods, surrendering his urge to fight. When he lifted his gaze once more, it was sharp and all-seeing, tracing the movements of both armies like strokes in a cosmic painting. Every signal he gave, every order shouted by his messengers, rippled across the battlefield with precision.

Beside Porus, Veerabhalla tore into the Macedonians with fearless abandon. His sword rose and fell like the striking of lightning, every motion cutting down another foe. Shoulder to shoulder, king and general became twin storms, devastating all who dared to stand before them.

On the far side of the battlefield, Alexander carved his own legend in blood and steel. Mounted atop Bucephalus—the black giant whose hooves struck like thunder and whose white blaze gleamed beneath the sun—the Macedonian king was a figure of near-divine terror. His sword flashed in his hand like a streak of white fire, each movement swift and precise, guided by years of mastery honed across continents. To his enemies, it seemed not a mortal blade but a bolt of lightning given to a man by Zeus himself.

Every strike carried catastrophic force. Macedonian steel cut through shield-lines, carving men apart as though their armor were paper reeds. Warriors split cleanly in half beneath his blows, their forms collapsing into the mud with sprays of blood and shattered bone. Entrails spilled onto the trampled earth, mixing with churned soil, forming rivers of gore where Bucephalus trampled forward. Screams rose, then broke into silence just as quickly, drowned by the relentless hammering chaos of war.

Fear, sharp and cold, swept through the lines of the Pauravas who faced him. They had never seen a man fight with such speed, such lethal rhythm, as if the very dance of death served his hand. He struck and struck again without pause, without falter. Where others tired as the battle raged, Alexander's movements seemed to grow sharper, faster, unrelenting. The sheen of blood upon his armor only made him more terrible to behold—an avenging war-god made flesh.

And yet, though trembling seized their hearts, not a single Paurava warrior gave ground. For they fought not merely as men—they fought as the shield of Aryavarta. Each defender saw beyond themselves: they saw their mothers and fathers, their children waiting at home, their fields, temples, and sacred rivers they swore to protect. Every arrow that flew, every spear thrusted at the invader, was not just for Porus, but for all they held holy.

To retreat, to falter, was to surrender not only their king but their gods, their land, their very soul as a people. Their deaths were certain should they fail, but their defiance was immortal if they stood. And so, even against the hellish sweep of Alexander's blade, they pressed forward into slaughter, roaring defiantly through the fear clawing at their hearts.

In that clash of blood and steel, two truths became clear to all who gazed upon the battlefield: Alexander fought like a force of Olympus unleashed upon the earth, and the Pauravas resisted with the hearts of a thousand lions, guardians who would not kneel even before the son of Zeus himself.

Alexander's movements were preternatural, faster than the eye could follow, each strike flowing seamlessly into the next with the precision of a master sculptor carving the shape of death. He fought as though the weight of armor and fatigue held no dominion over him, his blade slicing through the chaos as effortlessly as a reed cutting water. To his enemies, there was a terrible illusion in his fighting—he seemed not to struggle, but to *play* with his sword, as though battle were not survival, but a game known only to him.

Every sweep of his arm turned shields into splintered wood, armor into scrap, and men into broken husks. His sword cleaved not with brute ferocity but with remarkable grace, gliding through flesh and bone as though the barriers offered no resistance. Blood sprayed in arcs, painting the air around him in wet crimson, yet Alexander pushed forward unstained by hesitation, each strike measured, deliberate, and executed with unnerving calm.

He seemed tireless, immune to exhaustion where others faltered. In the haze of blood and screams, he stood like a flame that refused to waver. His rage was not wild or reckless but controlled, precise—an iron discipline married with unyielding wrath. Every stab, every cut, every parry carried intent, a surgeon's accuracy bound with a war-god's fury. And wherever he rode, his men followed with renewed vigor. The Macedonians, already hardened by conquests across Asia, now felt themselves indomitable with Alexander at their head. His very presence pressed courage into their veins, steadying their shields, quickening their spears, sharpening their cries. They surged like a wave behind him, the phalanx extending its deadly forest once more, cavalry wheeling in perfect discipline, striking wherever space was torn open.

Against this rising storm, the Pauravas—though fierce and unrelenting—began to bend. They did not break, for their hearts were of iron and their cause was sacred, but the sheer grinding weight of Macedonian discipline, sharpened by their king's godlike fury, pushed them back step by step. Lines wavered, formations buckled, men fell screaming beneath sword and sarissa alike.

The battlefield itself seemed to acknowledge Alexander's dominance. Where he went, the tide swelled. Around him, the dust of the Hydaspes rose like a cloak, the sunlight flashing on his armor as if Zeus himself blessed the advance. To friend and foe alike, he was no longer just a king—he was destiny incarnate, pressing inexorably forward, shaping the very world by the edge of his blade.

The Greeks pressed their advantage. Step by step, shield by shield, they seemed to carve open a path through the Indian lines. For a moment, it looked as though Alexander's destiny might indeed crush the defenders.

But then Rajaguru, watching from his command post, lifted his staff high. His voice thundered above the chaos:

"Loose the storm! Let them taste the wrath of Aryavarta!"

Chapter 36 – Rain of Arrows

At the signal of the Rajaguru, the forests on either flank erupted with hidden firepower. Thousands of Paurava archers, concealed in the thick shadows of trees and branches, loosed their volleys in perfect coordination. The sky darkened as though the heavens themselves had opened—not with rain, but with a storm of death.

The arrows did not fall randomly; each shot carried precision, drawn from months of training and Rajaguru's foresight. Arrows pierced Greek horses, collapsing cavalry riders into the dust. Arrows struck commanders who raised their voices, silencing them. Arrows sank into the tightly packed ranks of infantry, tearing gaps in the once-impenetrable phalanx. Macedonians shouted in sudden panic, their formations breaking as they searched for an enemy they could not even see. To them, it seemed as if the skies betrayed them, showering iron rain without form or face.

Alexander himself stood like a figure carved out of destiny, untouched by the chaos that swallowed lesser men. Arrows poured down in torrents, shrieking through the air like messengers of death, but his blade was everywhere, flashing arcs of steel that split them mid-flight. Sparks crackled as wood met bronze, each shattered shaft tumbling to the mud before it could reach him. It seemed impossible—one man against the very sky's wrath—yet Alexander moved with the unwavering calm of one who believed himself chosen by the gods.

At his side, Bucephalus proved no less a legend than his master. The great stallion moved with a grace both animal and divine, weaving between falling shafts with uncanny precision. His muscles rippled with coiled power as he sidestepped volleys by the slimmest of margins, hooves churning the ground in a rhythm that seemed born of instinct as much as memory. This was not mere training, but survival built over countless fields of war. From Chaeronea to Gaugamela, across Persian deserts and Bactrian mountains, Bucephalus had carried Alexander through storms of arrows, showers of javelins, and the chaos of a thousand cavalry charges. Here, too, he danced with death—and death faltered.

To watching eyes, horse and rider did not appear as separate beings but as one form—fused by years of shared peril, iron will, and unbreakable trust. When Alexander leaned left, Bucephalus bent with him; when the horse twisted right, the king's sword struck in the same motion, deflecting danger before it even fell. Their rhythm was seamless, beyond coordination—it was communion.

In the din of war, amidst the screams of men and elephants alike, Alexander's connection to Bucephalus was his one constant. He had generals he respected, soldiers he trusted—but none whom he loved as he loved this stallion. Bucephalus was not merely a mount; he was a companion, a brother-in-arms, a piece of Alexander's very soul forged in battle. The conqueror might one day lose men, lands, or empires, but he could not imagine losing this one creature who had carried him unflinching through the crucible of fate.

And so, together they moved through the storm like an omen, a vision of invincibility—man and beast defying the will of heaven itself, cleaving arrows from the sky as though they were but threads cast before a blade. In that moment, even the gods might have paused, watching the young king of Macedon and his immortal steed carve their path through the storm of doom without suffering a single touch from its hand.

But even Alexander's skill could not shield the thousands around him. The ground soon glistened with blood as Greek soldiers fell in heaps. Horses screamed in agony, collapsing and trapping riders beneath their writhing bodies. Units wavered as death multiplied. If this storm continued, the Macedonian army would be broken.

Yet Alexander's mind, sharp as his blade, raced with calculation. Around him, some of his commanders survived by ordering desperate measures: soldiers pressed shields above their heads, overlapping them until they created great iron shelters, tent-like structures of protection. This offered scant safety from the storm, but enough for breath to return to their lungs. Within one such turtle-formation, King Ambhi hunched low, his ambition and fear locking in battle within his chest.

"We must burn them out!" Ambhi's voice cracked like a whip, sharp and urgent over the din of battle. His eyes blazed with a mixture of fear and fury as he glanced toward the sky-darkening hail of arrows. "Cut the forest from its roots with flame! The archers are cowards, hiding in the branches. They think themselves invisible, untouchable. Burn their refuge," he snarled, "and their safety burns with it!"

The Macedonian officers glanced at one another, their faces taut with unease. The great oil vats—heavy stores dragged painstakingly from far western lands—were not meant for this. Every soldier knew their purpose: to pour upon the charging elephants, setting their hides ablaze, breaking their line before tusks shattered the phalanx. To waste that precious weapon now was to strip themselves naked before the gravest threat yet to come. Murmurs rippled among the commanders, voices dropping to harsh whispers between the clatter of shields.

"If we expend it now…" one began.

"…the elephants will be unstoppable," another finished grimly.

But Ambhi would not yield. He surged forward inside the shield-shelter, his face glistening with sweat. His voice rose, sharp with desperation, every syllable cutting at their faltering resolve.

"Better to have a chance against the elephants tomorrow than to die like helpless animals this very breath!" he thundered. "Do you not see? If this storm of arrows continues, we will not live for the beasts to trample us—the forest itself will bury us in death! Burn them now, or none of us will see another dawn!"

The words tore through hesitation like a blade. Messengers carried his command. Within moments, the decision reached Alexander himself.

The King of Macedon listened without outward emotion, his eyes fixed upon the fire-lit chaos of the battlefield. He weighed costs in silence, his mind whirring with the ruthless calculus of survival. To save men now was to risk greater loss later; to delay meant watching his army crumble under an invisible enemy. Destiny allowed no pause.

At last, Alexander gave the nod. Small and unassuming, yet to thousands it was the most terrible gesture they could imagine. “Do it,” he said curtly.

The order exploded through the Macedonian lines like a second war cry. Soldiers rushed to the stores, cracking open the oil vats. The stench of pitch and resin filled the air as flasks were dipped and prepared. Torches glowed in trembling hands, hungry fire dancing atop their heads.

Then they hurled them.

Flames arced across the battlefield, shattering upon the forest floor. A moment of silence followed—then the Hydaspes grove erupted in an inferno.

The green canopy was consumed in an instant, leaves crackling into ash, bark splitting with thunderous pops as fire raced up tree-trunks. Branches writhed in the heat like serpents aflame, and black smoke coiled skyward in great choking pillars. The cries of archers trapped among the boughs ripped the air—screams of agony that even the din of battle could not mask. Some leapt in desperation, their bodies tumbling, shattering upon the earth below. Those who survived the fall were cut down before they could rise, Macedonian steel hungrily feasting on their broken forms. Others burned alive where they clung, a ghastly chorus of shrieks rising into the sooty skies.

The Paurava ambush, so carefully orchestrated, so deadly, was carved into horror by fire. What had begun as a rain of arrows now became a rain of bodies—falling, shrieking,

writhing shadows set aflame. Beneath the canopy, the Hydra of Aryavarta was ablaze.
And Alexander, gazing across the smoke-choked plain, knew the tide had turned—for now.

But not all met death with fear.

Among the burning trunks, where the canopy shrieked with crackling fire and ash rained down like curses, a young Paurava archer clung to his perch. The flames embraced him like a merciless cloak, devouring his skin, searing his flesh, yet still he did not falter. His hands blistered, his lips cracked from the heat, but his bow was steady. His resolve burned brighter than the flames that sought to consume him.
The boy's mind drifted to the face of his father, clear even through the haze of agony. A weathered farmer turned soldier, cut down without mercy when Ambhi's betrayal opened their land to Macedonian blades. He remembered his mother's broken sobs the night his father's ashes were gathered, and the oath he had whispered silently into the stillness: *I shall not rest until the foreigner pays in blood.*
Now, as the fire devoured him, that memory became his shield. Grief and vengeance fused into a single, unquenchable flame. Every breath was agony, every heartbeat a hammer of pain—but still he drew, still he loosed. Arrows hissed downward in deadly rain, guided by hands that no longer feared death. His shafts pierced Greek helmets, felled horsemen from their mounts, and shattered through the shields of men who thought the fire had silenced the Pauravas. His screams of pain mingled with the twang of his bowstring until they became one sound—the cry of a soul burning but not broken.
Greeks looked up in horror to see a figure entirely wreathed in fire, a phantom of ash and flame unleashing death even as his body crumbled. Some thought he was no mortal at all, but a spirit of the forest unleashed by the gods.

One by one, his arrows struck true. One by one, enemies fell at the feet of his agony. At last, his legs gave way, charred muscle refusing the command of a will that still fought. His bow slipped from his hands. His body, now little more than burning flesh and bone, toppled forward from the tree. He fell like a comet, blazing, crashing among the dead already littering the ground. The weight of his fall broke his frame, and before he could draw breath again, he was trampled beneath men and horses.

His valor went unseen in the storm of war, his name lost to the smoke. His sacrifice was unrecorded, swallowed by the agony of thousands. Yet in that brief moment, in the fire and fury of his last defiance, the nameless archer stood as tall as any king—his arrows a testament that Aryavarta would not yield easily, even in death.

Rajaguru, watching from his vantage, felt his heart tighten. For a moment, even the master of strategy faltered, struck by the brutality of war. Then his resolve returned, harder than iron. His voice thundered across the Paurava lines:

“Unleash the elephants! Douse the flames with water from the sacred reservoirs! Let our titans trample both the fire and the enemy beneath their unstoppable might!”

At once, trumpets of war resounded. War elephants, fully armored, stormed forward like divine mountains in motion. At their sides surged mahouts guiding them to the reservoirs dug earlier—a gift of foresight. Buckets of water were flung from their towers, spraying across the burning groves. Other elephants simply ripped trees from the ground and crushed them beneath their weight, snuffing the fire with sheer force. The forest burned, yet the flames met living towers too powerful to be checked.

The scattering Greeks froze in horror as the beasts advanced. Many men trembled, dropping spears as shadows fell upon them. The sheer sight of tusks capped with steel and trunks raised high crushed courage from their hearts. Some men ran, only to be flattened under colossal hooves. Others fought, but their blades glanced harmlessly off the armored hides. The elephants ploughed through them as if through stalks of grain.

Above, archers who survived the inferno scrambled onto the beasts, raining arrows anew from the great living towers. The battlefield cried out with terror and fury as elephants crushed, impaled, and roared through Macedonian formations.

Alexander beheld the chaos with wide eyes. Part of him—the conqueror, the warrior—was exhilarated. Never before had he faced war in such brutal magnificence. It was terrifying, yes, but also intoxicating. "This is no ordinary campaign," he whispered to himself. "This is history."

And yet, even his awe could not hide the danger. The elephants were tearing his army apart, their rampage unchecked. Then his eyes sharpened with ruthless clarity. He knew the truth of war: cut the head, the body falls. Kill Porus, and all Aryavarta would break.

Raising his voice above the storm, Alexander commanded: "Ambhi! Commanders! Hold the elephants! Distract them, burn them, do whatever you must! I will not fight beasts when the king himself is the greater prize. I go for Porus!"

He gathered three or four of his finest commanders, men whose skill matched his own, and spurred Bucephalus forward. The black stallion leapt into motion, cutting through the chaos of flame, smoke, and dust.

Alexander's destiny now was clear: find Porus, and end the war with a single strike.

Chapter 37 – The Death of Bucephalus

Alexander had given his command. Ambhi and the Macedonian captains were to contain the rampaging elephants at all costs, while he himself, with a handful of his best commanders, rode directly toward Porus. His mind was clear—cut down the king, and the body of Aryavarta would fall lifeless.

Ambhi obeyed, rallying his men to fight with desperate resolve. Yet fate had other plans for him.
Through the frenzy of dust and steel came Veerabhalla, his blade dripping with blood, his eyes burning with unshakable fury. As he cleaved a path through enemies, his gaze locked upon Ambhi. Rage lit both their faces red, as old grudges rose amidst the greater war.
Ambhi knew this reckoning had waited too long. Veerabhalla, the sword-arm of Porus, had humiliated Taxila in the past, crushing Ambhi's forces when he had betrayed his Aryavarta kin. Now, amid the flames of Hydaspes, they stood face-to-face again.
"Traitor!" Veerabhalla roared, his voice echoing like a storm. "How dare you betray your own motherland? Do you not smell the ashes of your ancestors, cursed by your cowardice?"
Ambhi spat back, hatred twisting his lips. "You speak of motherland as if it will shield me from death! My life is paramount—more than land, more than people. What good is loyalty when a grave waits at its end?"
Their blades met with a ringing clash that drowned the chaos around them. Sparks flew, steel shrieked. Ambhi fought with desperation, but desperation cannot match experience. Veerabhalla moved like the embodiment of war itself—his strikes precise, his strength inexorable. With each clash, Ambhi stumbled back, his defenses wearing thin.
At last, a furious downward stroke smashed through his guard. Ambhi's sword split from his hand, his chest opening before the killing blow. Veerabhalla's eyes burned with righteous rage as his blade drove deep. Ambhi gasped, eyes wide, then crumpled onto the earth—his life draining, his betrayal extinguished.

The battlefield seemed to pause at the fall of the Taxilan king. Macedonian and Paurava soldiers alike glanced in shock. One of Alexander's allies lay dead, struck down not by Porus, but by the sword of his fiercest general. Veerabhalla's vengeance thundered no words—he simply raised his bloodied blade high, rallying his men once more. But in that breath of calm, he realized Alexander himself was gone from the chaos. The King of Macedon was not among the elephants or the flanks. He had gone ahead—to Porus. At once, Veerabhalla carved through enemies anew, desperate to reach his king's side.
Meanwhile, Alexander's passage cut straight through the Paurava lines. No man escaped his blade. Soldiers fell in heaps, arrows clanged harmlessly as he advanced, pressing forward until the towering form of Porus loomed before him. And in that instant, the two kings met.

Alexander's eyes widened—not in fear, but in awe. For before him stood not a mere king of a distant land, not a chieftain raised up by circumstance, but a figure who seemed carved from the very bedrock of Aryavarta itself. Porus loomed taller than any man Alexander had ever faced, his towering frame encased in gleaming armor that caught the sun and refracted it like a halo of fire. Atop his elephant he seemed not mortal, but a titan descended from heaven—an equal to Heracles, perhaps even to Achilles, the heroes Alexander had always aspired to surpass.

Every movement Porus made revealed not just strength, but a majesty sharpened upon countless trials of rule and war. His muscles rippled with power, yet his motions carried the disciplined grace of one who wielded weapons as naturally as others wield words. The great bow in his hand bent easily to his draw, the spear balanced in his grip as though weightless, and the sword at his side gleamed hungrily, eager to taste

blood. The smoke and fury of the battlefield did not conceal his power—it magnified it. Porus was one of those rare men whose stature grew in the crucible of chaos, revealed in moments where others shrank in fear.
Alexander, who had stormed Thebes, who had slain Darius' armies and shattered Persia's pride, who had marched to the very ends of the known world without bowing to any foe—felt, for the first time in many years, the stirrings of genuine surprise within his heart. Awe, pure and undeniable, bound him as he looked upon the king of Paurava.
Here was no petty monarch to be cowed, no mercenary general clinging to hollow bravado. Here was a counterpart—a rival forged by destiny itself. Porus fought with the wrath of gods, but bore himself with the restraint and dignity of a true sovereign.
And Alexander, hardened by a thousand battlefields, could not deny what he saw: in Porus, he faced not simply an obstacle to empire, but the mirror of his own greatness.

Porus too regarded him, and for a fleeting moment, the battlefield seemed to fade the cries of men, the clash of steel, even the thunder of elephants and horses dimmed—as his eyes met those of the Macedonian king. What he saw there was not merely an invader, but something that stirred deep recognition within him.

Alexander was young, but his gaze was ancient, carved with victories and sacrifice. His bearing radiated command, his swordplay spoke of discipline forged in fire. Porus, who had seen countless men come and go, who had faced both loyalty and betrayal, who had lived among kings whose ambitions rarely matched their courage—recognized in Alexander a kindred soul. Brave. Unyielding. Masterful in both war and will.

It was as if two rivers, born worlds apart, had finally converged to crash against each other. One, the Ganga of Aryavarta, ancient and sacred; the other, the flood of the West, young and unstoppable. Perhaps, in another life, their waters might have mingled peacefully. In another life, they might have stood side by side—kings, warriors, brothers in ambition, bound not by conquest but by respect.

Porus' heart swelled for a breath with something rare upon the battlefield: admiration. This foreign king, unlike the treacherous Ambhi or the arrogant lords he had crushed before, was not a man hiding behind deceit or borrowed strength. No—this was a warrior who bled truth with every swing of his sword. A man who carved his empire with his own hands, not through cowardice but through sheer might and vision.

But destiny is a cruel arbiter. The gods, in their inscrutable will, had not cast them as allies, but as rivals—bound to test each other's mettle in the forge of war. Their admiration, therefore, could not bloom into brotherhood. It had to be measured in arrows, spears, and blood. Respect was there, unspoken, blazing in both their eyes—but it was respect chained to enmity.

So Porus, towering upon his mighty elephant, tightened his grip upon his bow. Alexander, astride Bucephalus, lowered his spear in reply. No words were shared—none were needed. Both men understood the truth: theirs was a meeting not of strangers, but of equals. And such men could only truly know each other through the final communion of war.

The first exchange came by bow.

Porus drew with the strength of a giant, his bow creaking like a thundercloud before the storm. Each arrow he loosed screamed through the air like lightning bolts hurled from Indra's own hand. They struck with devastating force, splintering shields, shattering the ground, rattling the very air around Alexander.

Yet Bucephalus, the black war-stallion bred for gods, moved with uncanny speed. He twisted and lunged sideways at the last instant, slipping through impossibly tight gaps as arrows slammed into the earth where Alexander had been a heartbeat before. To all watching, it was as though the horse and rider shared a single mind—one anticipating, the other evading, flowing in perfect unison.

In turn, Alexander's bow snapped taut with deadly precision. His arrows hissed like serpents, swift and sharp, finding gaps in the armor of Porus' elephant. But the Indian king raised his massive shield, deflecting shaft after shaft with an ease that belied his towering size. The arrows clanged against bronze and iron, harmless as splinters against a wall. Porus' face betrayed no fear; his eyes burned brighter the more he deflected, his focus narrowing only upon the Macedonian ahead of him.

Even as the arrows flew, their mounts themselves joined the battle.

Porus' mighty elephant surged forward, trumpeting so loudly that the earth seemed to quake. Its tusks gored the air in savage arcs, each swing a battering ram of living ivory meant to crush man and horse alike. Its colossal feet stamped the bloodied ground, leaving deep craters as it pressed forward—a moving fortress, a god-beast at war.

Bucephalus answered with the defiance of a creature who had never known defeat. The black stallion reared high upon his hindlegs, hooves lashing like hammer-blows of iron. With astonishing reflexes, he dodged beneath the swiping tusks, pivoting left, then right, the muscles beneath his sleek coat straining with barely contained fury. Sparks flew where tusk met earth, while the stallion struck back—hooves slamming against the elephant's trunk, forcing it to recoil for precious seconds.

Man against man, beast against beast—the duel had narrowed the battle to a single point of fate. Thousands clashed across the Hydaspes plain, but here, in the center, existence itself seemed to pause and stare. Every arrow shot, every cry of beast, every thundering step shook the ground as if two worlds collided—East and West, Aryavarta and Macedon, dharma and destiny.

Neither gave quarter, neither relented. Porus and Alexander fought not only with the mastery of their arms but with the sheer force of *being* . Both knew that this struggle was larger than them, larger than their armies. It was a duel the ages themselves demanded—a meeting fated not for men, but for legends.

Suddenly, Alexander's keen eyes caught sight of a spear half-buried in the churned earth, abandoned by some fallen soldier. With a surge of instinct, he seized it, his fingers curling around the shaft as though guided by Fate itself. Rising upon Bucephalus' back, he channeled every ounce of wrath, grief, and unbending will into that single motion.

With the strength of fury, born from years of conquest stretching across three continents, Alexander hurled the spear. The weapon tore through the air with a scream that silenced the clamor of battle, streaking across the no-man's space between titan and conqueror. It was no mere weapon—it was an arrow of destiny, a thunderbolt that would decide the day.

But Porus was no ordinary foe. His reflexes—unnatural in their swiftness for a warrior of such size—flared like lightning. His hand shot up, immense fingers gripping the wooden shaft even as it sped toward his chest. The force of impact rattled the giant king's arm, yet he held firm, twisting the deadly javelin off its course.

For a heartbeat, silence fell. Warriors froze, breath locked in their throats as they beheld the impossible—Porus, the mountain of Aryavarta, had caught the spear of Alexander in mid-flight. Then with a roar that shook both armies, Porus turned, his own muscles straining as he reeled the spear back. In one sweeping motion, he hurled it back with vengeance. The air split anew, but now the deadly shaft sang with double the fury, as though its breath carried voices of both kings locked within it.

Alexander reacted instantly, his body twisting with trained precision. The spear brushed past his side by the breadth of a thread, grazing the wind from his shoulder. For a fleeting instant he thought himself escaped.

But destiny had other marks.

Bucephalus, faithful titan of the West, could not evade what his rider barely dodged. The spear struck true, plunging deep into the stallion's chest. A wet, sickening crunch followed as iron pierced muscle and tore through the heart that had carried Alexander since boyhood.

The mighty horse reared violently, its agonized shriek rising above the clash of elephants and men, echoing like a soul ripped from the earth itself. Foam mixed with blood at its lips as its proud eyes, once blazing with fire, dimmed in pain. The beast staggered, legs trembling beneath its immense weight.

Alexander screamed his mount's name, the first crack of anguish in a voice otherwise unbroken by years of war, but it was too late. Bucephalus gave one final, shuddering cry, then collapsed with cataclysmic force. The ground quaked beneath his fall, dust billowing into the air.

The black stallion—the shadow that had borne Alexander across deserts, mountains, rivers, and kingdoms—lay still, his massive weight crashing down upon his master.

Alexander was hurled beneath him, the horse's body pinning his legs with its full, crushing weight.

The conqueror, the man who had bent empires to his will, now lay trapped beneath the dying heartbeat of his only true companion.

Alexander's scream tore across the field, louder than the clash of shields, louder than the trumpet of elephants. As Bucephalus collapsed upon him, his massive ribs shattered and his lifeblood soaking the dust, the king of Macedon lay pinned beneath the weight of his oldest companion. His legs were crushed, muscles torn beneath the colossal burden, yet his voice cracked not with his own agony—but with anguish deeper than any wound of flesh.

"Bucephalus!" he cried, his words breaking like a child's sob. "My brother, my shadow!"

Tears streaked his face, cutting through dust and blood, the mask of a conqueror stripped away in an instant. His hands clawed desperately at the dark, sweat-slickened body of his horse, fingernails bleeding as he tried to move what could not be moved. His armor scraped against flesh as he pulled, as though he could will life back into the dying giant. Blood poured warm from the wound in Bucephalus' chest, soaking Alexander's arms, filling his palms, staining his armor in rivers of red.

It was not the blood of a mere beast—it was the last strength of his most loyal companion, the only soul who had carried him undefeated across deserts, mountains, and rivers, through storms of javelins and showers of arrows, through the rise and fall of countless kings. Bucephalus had never betrayed him. Never faltered. Never feared. And now, as gods and mortals watched, the stallion that had borne a world conqueror breathed its final breaths upon him.

The battlefield itself seemed to stagger, as though time recoiled at the sight. Macedonians gasped; even hardened veterans faltered in their step when they saw Alexander crushed beneath the body of his dying steed. A ripple spread through both armies—shock, pity, awe. For the first time, the Son of Zeus, the King of Macedon, lay helpless. Not brought low by blade or warrior, but by the cruel hand of fate striking at his heart.

His commanders rushed forward in alarm, their shields snapping together in a wall of steel around him, arrows clattering harmlessly against their formation. They fended off every rush and strike, desperate to keep their king from being overwhelmed. But even before their protective circle had fully closed, fate struck again.

From the chaos, somewhere unseen, an arrow hissed. It cut the smoke and struck Alexander in the shoulder. He groaned, his head snapping to the side, blood seeping from the wound in thick rivulets. The pain was sharp, stabbing, but he barely gave it notice. His hand still clung to the thick mane of Bucephalus, his fingers twined in the coarse hair like a child afraid to let go of his dying parent.

No cry of rage burst from him, no command of war thundered from his lips. He ignored the screams of battle and the ring of blades surrounding him. His voice now was not that of a general or of a king—it was that of a grieving man, whispering broken words no one else could hear, spoken only to the horse whose ears had known his secrets since youth.

The conqueror of Persia. The crusher of cities. The man the Greeks called divine. In this moment, he was none of these.

He was only Alexander—the boy who had tamed a wild stallion as a child, a bond that had outlived generals, friends, and lovers. Now brought low, not by defeat, but by sorrow.

From atop his towering elephant, Porus beheld the sight before him—Alexander pinned beneath the lifeless body of Bucephalus, bloodied and broken, his anguished cries echoing over the tumult of war. In that instant, Porus' heart, mighty with wrath and fire, steadied itself. What he saw was not the vaunted son of Zeus nor the invader of Aryavarta—

but a man entrapped beneath fate, grieving for his brother-beast.

Without hesitation, Porus raised his hand. His booming voice carried across the thunder of battle:

"Halt."

The great elephant obeyed, pausing with tusks lowered, as if it too understood its master's command. The king of Paurava descended slowly, his massive sandals striking the earth with a sound as heavy as the beat of war drums. His figure—towering still even without the beast—marched straight through the chaos. Arrows hissed past him, swords gleamed in the periphery, but Porus did not falter. Soldiers, stunned by the sheer force of his presence, gave way instinctively.

Soon, he stood before Alexander. The Macedonian commanders, desperate, lowered their spears in warning, their eyes burning with both fear and devotion. But Porus stride did not break, nor did his head lower. He fixed them with a gaze that spoke louder than a hundred words—the gaze of a sovereign who commanded not just soldiers, but fate itself.

At last, he lifted his palm, halting only a stride away. His voice rang out, heavy, regal, unshakable—the voice of a king whose honor outweighed wrath:

"I cannot slay an enemy who is unarmed, pinned, and broken."

The words rolled out like a decree, carrying to ears far beyond the circle of guards. Silence rippled outward, capturing even the roar of war in its sweep.

"Your king bleeds, yet he does not wield. He lies crushed, mourning, not fighting. To strike him now would feed victory but rob honor. I will not mar my crown with such blood."

Porus' voice lowered, yet carried such authority that none dared move. His hand swept toward the fallen Alexander.

"Take him. Tend him. Let him heal. When he is mended and stands upon his own feet, then destiny may speak between us again."

For a heartbeat, time froze. Macedonian guards stared, torn between disbelief and awe. To kill their king's enemy when gods themselves had delivered him broken into their grasp would mean an easy triumph. But here was Porus, the enemy they had feared, extending not blade but mercy. Something shifted across the battlefield; even the clash of swords faltered, men pausing, compelled by the weight of the moment.

Porus turned, his cloak swirling, and strode back toward his elephant. In that instant, the king of Paurava seemed greater than any conqueror—for he had defeated not only his foe, but his own fury. That act, bearing the mark of dharma itself, would echo long beyond the Hydaspes: the day when one king refused to dishonor another, even with victory at his feet.

The Macedonian guards, stunned by the mercy of the man they had come to kill, lifted Alexander from beneath Bucephalus' body. His unconscious form was borne back across the Hydaspes, together with the body of his horse. Word spread swiftly across the battlefield—Alexander had fallen, Porus had spared him.

The war stilled. Trumpets faded. Both sides, stunned by the spectacle of mercy, pulled back. The Macedonians retreated to their camp, mourning losses and burying the dead. Among them, too, Ambhi was cremated, the traitor honored as comrade in death despite whispers of betrayal. The Pauravas returned to their camp, tending to wounded, performing final rites for their slain.

And in Alexander's pavilion, silence reigned. The king lay unconscious, his wound treated, his body resting. Outside, his men buried Bucephalus—the horse who had carried the conqueror across half the world—his grave dug with reverence, his name spoken with tears.

The river Hydaspes ran quiet that night, carrying with it the echoes of a battle where neither army claimed full victory. Yet in that silence lingered the promise of destiny unfulfilled: a duel between two kings, interrupted but not ended.

Chapter 38 – The End of the War

The days after the battle were heavy with silence. The proud figure of Alexander, once an unstoppable force, lay motionless upon his bed of furs, his body broken by grief and wounds alike. The death of Bucephalus had shattered his spirit as no blade or arrow ever had. His shoulder burned from the arrow lodged deep, his legs ached under the memory of the crushing weight, but it was his heart that bore the deepest wound. The conqueror of Persia, the son of hellenic pride, now lay still, breathing but unmoving, as though his will itself had been buried alongside his beloved horse.

His commanders, men hardened by campaigns across the world, waited anxiously. Days turned into nights, nights into a week. Each morning, they entered his tent hoping the king would stir, rise, and thunder his next order, to point the way toward victory. But Alexander remained silent—the young lion who had roared across continents, lying now with closed eyes, trapped somewhere between life and shadow.
In the camp around him, the Macedonians began to unravel. For the first time, cracks tore open in their unity. Soldiers groaned in desperation, the dream of endless conquest withering in their hearts. Many had crossed deserts, mountains, and rivers with their king. They had fought beneath foreign suns year after year. But now, after facing

death in the land of Porus—facing mauling elephants, fire, traps, arrows—there was no more taste for glory.

Whispers filled the campfires: *home.* Wives, children, farms, hearths—the things they had abandoned long ago. They had fought enough, bled enough, buried enough brothers along the roads of conquest. Now men wept quietly at night, longing for embraces more than riches, safe laughter more than towers of gold. They realized with bitter clarity that fame and wealth meant nothing when one's bones were trampled nameless in a land thousands of miles from Greece.

At last, after a week had passed, there was still no word from their king. Some believed he would never rise again. The commanders bowed to the inevitable. They drew together and sent word to Porus.

The scroll was carried under a flag of truce, its words solemn and humble:

"The war is ended. We have no more strength to fight. Your valor was unmatched, your kindness has been seen by us all. To follow you into battle was to be taught by you. King Alexander's fall and your mercy have shown us more than victory could. We thank you, noble king of Paurava. Let the land heal, as we retreat to our homes."

When Porus received the message, he felt the weight that had shadowed him for weeks lift at last. He read the letter aloud to Rajaguru, to Veerabhalla, and to his council. To his people he announced: *"The invader returns, and Aryavarta stands free."* Joy blossomed across the kingdom. Farmers who had hidden in fear returned to their fields. Wives performed rites for the fallen. The sons of Paurava greeted their king not only as victor, but as protector.

Porus sent blessings in return, praising the Macedonians for their courage, Alexander for his brilliance, and admiring even their stubborn tenacity. Yet he reminded his people: it was not just his sword that saved them, but the wisdom of Rajaguru, the strength of Veerabhalla, and the sacrifice of countless nameless warriors whose blood sealed the land from foreign rule.

The kingdom of Paurava began to heal.

Meanwhile, in the Macedonian camp, preparations were made to depart. But before leaving, a whisper stirred in Alexander's tent. One of his generals leaned close, and with a voice faint as wind upon reeds, the king spoke. His lips trembled with his final command of remembrance:

"Name this place… for him. For Bucephalus. Let the city bear his name… where we buried him."

His generals, their eyes moist with grief, obeyed. A city rose upon the banks of the Hydaspes—Bucephala—etched into the map of the world so that future ages would remember the bond between a conqueror and his faithful horse.

At last, the army began the long road westward. Their march took them across rivers and deserts, toward the heartlands of their empire. But the world conqueror did not see his home again. In Babylon, fever claimed Alexander, and the breath left his lungs for the final time. The man who dreamed of eternity was laid to rest in Egypt, in the city he himself had founded—Alexandria—a monument to his ambition and his endless will.

The invincible conqueror fell. Yet beyond his empire, beyond his victories, his story remained forever bound to another's: the battle where he faced King Porus of Aryavarta—his rival, his equal, and the man who spared him.

Enjoyed this story?

If the journey of King Porus and his epic stand against Alexander stirred your imagination, I invite you to explore my other novel, ***Krishna: The Paradox of Dharma .***

This novel dives deep into the life of Krishna—not just as a divine hero but as a complex being wrestling with the weight and contradictions of Dharma itself. It is a tale of devotion

and doubt, power and compassion, where gods question their own mandates and heroes face impossible choices.
Step beyond history and myth into a world where divine order is challenged, and resistance is born not from rebellion, but from the paradoxes of righteousness.
Discover a new epic of ancient India—rich with philosophy, drama, and the timeless struggle between duty and free will.
If you found yourself captivated by this story, *Krishna: The Paradox of Dharma* awaits you. Thank you for reading.
— Ledalla Naga Sai Adhi Vishnu

www.ingramcontent.com/pod-product-compliance
Ingram Content Group UK Ltd.
Pitfield, Milton Keynes, MK11 3LW, UK
UKHW041314190726
13845UKWH00025B/249

9 789334 387421